THE END OF THE STORY

Biblioasis International Translation Series
General Editor: Stephen Henighan

Since 2007 the Biblioasis International Translation Series has been publishing exciting literature from Europe, Latin America, Africa and the minority languages of Canada. Committed to the idea that translations must come from the margins of linguistic cultures as well as from the power centres, the Biblioasis International Translation Series is dedicated to publishing world literature in English in Canada. The editors believe that translation is the lifeblood of literature, that a language that is not in touch with other linguistic traditions loses its creative vitality, and that the worldwide spread of English makes literary translation more urgent now than ever before.

I Wrote Stone: The Selected Poetry of Ryszard Kapuściński (Poland)
        Translated by Diana Kuprel and Marek Kusiba

Good Morning Comrades by Ondjaki (Angola)
        Translated by Stephen Henighan

Kahn & Engelmann by Hans Eichner (Austria-Canada)
        Translated by Jean M. Snook

Dance With Snakes by Horacio Castellanos Moya (El Salvador)
        Translated by Lee Paula Springer

Black Alley by Mauricio Segura (Quebec)
        Translated by Dawn M. Cornelio

The Accident by Mihail Sebastian (Romania)
        Translated by Stephen Henighan

Love Poems by Jaime Sabines (Mexico)
        Translated by Colin Carberry

The End of the Story by Liliana Heker (Argentina)
        Translated by Andrea G. Labinger

Liliana Heker

THE END OF
THE STORY

TRANSLATED FROM THE SPANISH
BY ANDREA G. LABINGER

BIBLIOASIS

Originally published as *El fin de la historia* by Alfaguara S.A., Buenos
Aires, Argentina, 1996.

FIRST EDITION

Library and Archives Canada Cataloguing in Publication

Heker, Liliana
    The end of the story / Liliana Heker ; translator, Andrea Labinger.

(Biblioasis international translation series)
Translation of: El fin de la historia.
ISBN 978-1-926845-48-7

    I. Labinger, Andrea G II. Title. III. Series: Biblioasis international
translation series

PQ7798.18.E44F5513 2012   863'.64   C2011-907874-0

Edited by Stephen Henighan.

We acknowledge the assistance of the Translation Support Program of
the Directorate of Cultural Affairs of the Argentine Foreign Ministry.

PRINTED AND BOUND IN USA

To Ernesto Imas

One

Anyone watching the olive-skinned woman walk along Montes de Oca that October afternoon would have thought that she had been born to drink life down to the bottom of the glass. It had to be true. Even those who would disparage her years later would have noticed it somehow, seeing her advance towards Suárez like someone who has always known exactly where she was going. Diana Glass herself, who at that very moment was sitting cross-legged on the floor of her balcony – eyes closed, face upturned to the sun like an offering – must have thought so because sometime later she would jot down in her notebook with the yellow pages: *She was born to drink life down to the bottom of the glass.* Although a certain ironic expression (or was it just wisdom enough to soften the expression, to de-emphasize it) crossed her mind like a bolt of malice: Is that necessarily a virtue?

She was tormented by these distractions, which, from her very first notation on a paper napkin at Café Tiziano, kept diverting the course of the story. Not to mention the reality that, from that napkin to this haven on the balcony, had flung her – one might say – from hope to horror, and which (though neither one of them knew it), at that moment when the olive-skinned woman unhesitatingly turned off Suárez, heading towards Isabel La Católica, would once again begin to unravel her tale.

Strictly speaking, Diana Glass, who now opened her eyes and gazed admiringly at a bougainvillea blooming on the opposite balcony, hadn't even decided where to begin: with the spring morning when a tree fell on her head and the two of them – or at least she – thought about death for the first time, or with a freezing, dusty July afternoon fourteen years later – when death had already begun to be a less remote eventuality, although it hadn't yet become that chill on the back of the neck every time one turned the key in the lock to enter one's house – as she waited nearly a half-hour for her at the entrance of the school, staring insistently towards the corner of Díaz Vélez and Cangallo so not to miss the elation – or the relief? – of seeing her arrive.

The name she was going to give her, on the other hand, was something she had decided right away. Leonora. Not because it had anything to do with her real name (less melodious), but rather because it went well with that face, with its high cheekbones and olive skin, still smiling at me from the last photo, and it suited that jaunty girl who, if Diana Glass had simply begun with that unpleasant July afternoon in 1971, would by now have burst out of Díaz Vélez onto the page, waving with such an old, familiar gesture that it would have made Diana forget her fear for a few seconds.

Later, it was different. The other woman had barely finished waving her arm, her features hazily coming into focus, when the relief would be replaced by a premonition of catastrophe.

It should be pointed out that Diana Glass is nearsighted and that, at the time of that meeting with Leonora, she refused to wear glasses. Her explanation was that the few things worth seeing in detail usually end up moving closer to you (or you to them) and besides, a nearsighted person's view doesn't just have the advantage of being polysemic: it is also incomparably more beautiful than a normal person's. "Just think about the sky after dark," she once said. "I swear, the first night I went out on the balcony wearing glasses, I almost cried. The real moon has no resemblance to that enormous, mystical halo I see." And, she added, the diffuse forms allow a limitless range of imagination, as if the world had been created by some over-the-top impressionist.

These are the sort of interruptions that disturbed her. (*Absurdity has invaded the story*, she wrote, though not in the notebook with yellow pages, which she reserved for episodes that were more or less relevant, but rather on the back of one of those printed ledger sheets that she haphazardly filled: papers with a predetermined function exempted her from assigning one to them herself and allowed her madness to spill out unrestrained. *Absurdity has invaded the story, has invaded History*. Nothing could be truer. She was plunging into History; perversely, doing so prevented her from dealing with the purely historical, despite her belief that history was the only thing that made any sense.) For example, she was unable to assess the exact quality of her fear at the school doorway (assuming, of course, that the fear was historical) without noting her surprise at the fact that the closer the woman got, the more unfamiliar she became, and how could she explain that phenomenon without mentioning her myopia? But if the beginning was hesitant, the ending was alarmingly blank. Nothing. Just a little faith and a few old photographs. And a very immediate fear lodging at the back of her head as she turned the key in the lock of her front door – and at this very moment – and didn't go with the light of this October afternoon in 1976, a light that illuminated the bougainvillea, adorned Buenos Aires, and mercilessly enhanced the olive skin of the woman who has now turned off Suárez and is heading towards Isabel La Católica.

The trees on Plaza Colombia catch her by surprise. It's as if something dangerously vital – more suitable to a jungle than to this grey street with its stone church – as if an unscrupulous thirst for life had forced them to overflow the plaza, invade the sidewalk of Isabel La Católica and bury the unfortunate Church of Santa Felícitas beneath an avalanche of joy.

She has one desire: not to go to the meeting at the house with the white door where Fernando, the Thrush, and two others must already be waiting for her, not suspecting the contents of one of the two letters she hides in the false bottom of her purse. To run away towards Plaza Colombia, that's her precise desire. This, however, doesn't disturb her, as the purple explosion of bougainvillea has disturbed Diana Glass to the point of forcing her to leave the balcony and walk to the library. *Both of them loved the sun*, she thinks, like someone who's writing it down (or like someone making excuses for herself) – as she did so often in those days – and she takes out the box with the photos of the trip to Mendoza.

There they are, the two of them. Among vineyards, on top of a stone block, on the shoulders of a couple of drunks, on a suspension bridge, thumbing their noses, in wide-brimmed hats, always laughing and embracing and a bit outrageous among the group of brand-new – and slightly foolish – schoolteachers.

The woman who at this moment is walking through the imitation jungle that spills out of Plaza Colombia lifts her head for a moment, allowing the sun filtering through the leaves to flicker on her face without thinking: I was born to drink life down to the bottom of the glass.

It might not displease her if someone else thought it for her. That's true! she would exclaim if she knew about this assessment of her person that Diana Glass is about to make. She knows how to delight in other people's words and put them at her service when necessary.

But she doesn't need to define herself in order to confirm her existence. Accustomed to action and to charging headlong at everything in her way, she knows she exists because her body (and what's a brain but a part of that body?) displaces the air as she moves, leaving an exact impression on the world. And if she hasn't slowed her pace, if she hasn't gone running towards Plaza Colombia, following her heart's song, if she's left the trees behind, guiltlessly abandoning this fleeting, intoxicating desire, if now, without a speck of desire, she's about to head proudly and resolutely towards Wenceslao Villafañe, it's because, even now when her world seems to be tumbling down, she's still capable of brushing aside all trivialities in the name of what she's convinced she needs to do.

♦

But with Celina Blech's arrival (when vacation ended, in the time of the tree), something began to change. Celina, too, had read Captains of the Sands *and had sung "The Army of the Ebro," but she possessed a quality Leonora and I lacked: she could unhesitatingly state who was a revolutionary and who was a counter-revolutionary. Heraclitus? she said. Heraclitus was a revolutionary, and Berkeley was, without a doubt, a reactionary. Listening to her was amazing: standing beside the bench, flanked by girls who crossed themselves before class and went to dances at the club with their mothers every Saturday, and by girls who neither crossed themselves nor took their mothers along to dances but who didn't seem too impressed by Heraclitus's revolutionary powers either, she had the guts, in front of the philosophy teacher, an active member of Catholic Action, to obliterate Berkeley with a swipe of her pen for his notorious inability to start a revolution. The daughter of a poetic Communist shoemaker of the old guard, she behaved with the confidence of someone who has always known where the world is going and who moves it. It was she who taught us to read Marx. How could anyone forget the leap of the heart, the jubilant certainty (for me, too) that the world was marching along a happy course, when reading for the first time that a spectre is haunting Europe ? And every week, concealed in an innocent-looking package, she brought us a copy of* Communist Youth *magazine.*

She never flaunted her superiority before Leonora or me – she was good-natured, a comrade, and she had little patience for the rock and roll that, despite "The Army of the Ebro" with its rumbalabumbalabumbambá and its Ay, Carmela, Leonora and I kept dancing to frenetically during our Saturday assaults – but that latent superiority was there, nonetheless, and soon it would become apparent. In all other respects we were similar: all three of us loved the Romantic poet Esteban Echeverría and despised Cornelio Saavedra, the head of Argentina's first junta; all three of us resonated to the verses of Nicolás Guillén; all three declared, with the élan of Spanish Republicans at the very moment of victory, that the invading troops rumbalabumbalabumbambá got a well-deserved trouncing, Ay, Carmela. So we sang and so we were that winter of 1958 when History invaded our peaceful Teachers' Prep School in the Almagro District.

Later we would learn that it had been there all along, that, without realizing it, we had noticed it among the small events woven by our personal memories. Chaotically and without any sign – or with some fortuitous sign – I preserved the memory of that morning in grade two when they made us leave school early because some general had tried to oust Perón (whom I imagined as eternal and omnipresent, since he had been in the world when I was born and since my mother had forbidden me to pronounce his name in vain); the slogan Free the Rosenbergs, read on the walls of forgotten streets; the outrage of some older cousins at the phrase "Boots, Yes; Books, No"; the hoarse voice of a news hawker shouting War in Korea; and a secret, incommunicable envy when, in the movie newsreel children who weren't me travelled through the Children's City by bus like fortunate dwarves; a certain initial disbelief in the face of death the day the Air Force bombed the Plaza de Mayo; an almost literary emotion when a group of men, in a hidden place called Sierra Maestra, prepared to free Cuba – a remote country about which only "The Peanut Vendor" and Blanquita Amaro's ebullient thighs were familiar to me; the bitter or dejected faces of some bricklayers one late September morning in 1955. Random fragments jumbled together in my memory, with the German acrobats around the Obelisk, with a butcher named Burgos who had scattered pieces of his girlfriend throughout Buenos Aires, with a nine-year-old girl who had drowned in Campana and who could be seen, brutally depicted at the moment she went under, on a page of La Razón. *Scraps of something whose ultimate shape seemed – continues to seem – impossible.*

And we would also come to know the dizzying sensation of imagining ourselves submerged in History. Because one day soon, reality would be shaped so that everything – I mean everything – that occurred on earth would be happening to us. The Cuban Revolution and the war in Vietnam would be ours; the antagonism between China and the Soviet Union and the distant echoes of men who, in the Americas or in Africa or in every oppressed corner of the planet, lifted their heads: all of it would be our business. We fleetingly attempted to figure out the meaning of our lives. And we would live with the startling revelation – and the strange reassurance – of understanding that the world could not do without our deeds.

But that was the end of the winter of 1958 when, as proper young students, we recited the lesson from Astolfi's History and sang that bombs are powerless *rumbalabumbalabumbambá* if you just have heart, *ay Carmela*; that September of 1958 when History came to Mohammed. It awakened the universities, shook the entire nation, invaded classrooms for the first time, and at the peaceful Teachers' Prep with its wisteria-covered patio, it left no stone unturned.

I wonder now if it might have been a gift, a blessing whose uniqueness we were unaware of: to be fifteen years old and to have a compelling cause. Everything seemed so clear that late winter and the following spring: on one side were the people, behind a goal as incontrovertible as universal education; on the other side, the government, allied with the power of the church in order to impose its dogmatic, elitist lesson. It didn't matter if the motives of either side were less than transparent. At fifteen, beneath the budding wisteria and with a motto that seemed to condense all possible good and evil for the species – secular and free, we said, confident that we were encompassing the universe – we believed we could confirm forever those words we read as though they were anointed: the people's cause is a righteous cause; all righteous causes lead to victory; we have a role to play in that road to victory.

The headiness of the struggle, combined with the golden wine of adolescence – wasn't that our touchstone, the stamp that marked us? I look around me on this particularly dark night in 1976 and can see only death and ravaged flesh, and yet I keep on stubbornly typing these words, perhaps because I can't tear hope from my heart. Because once you've tasted that early wine, you cannot, do not want to give it up.

I see I've gotten mired in melancholy, but that wasn't what I wanted to talk about. I wanted to talk about certain domestic problems.

We've already established that there were three of us muses, three of us in the vanguard, and that our task was nothing less than to rouse a group of nice, future schoolteachers who hadn't asked to be roused and who, more than anything else, aspired to matrimony. It wasn't easy. Personally, I can say that I killed myself haranguing those young hordes, prodding them to organize and strike. I closed the eyes of my soul and hurled myself headlong into the jumble of my prose. Only in this way could I fulfill my mission. Because if I stopped for one second to reflect, I risked reaching a conclusion that would render me silent: I had no faith that my words could change a single one of those heads turned towards me with detached curiosity. In other words, my political career was in doubt. Leonora, on the other hand . . . That September, dressed in her white school smock, she revealed herself to us like a Pasionaria. She spoke, and Argentina became a burning rose, crying out for justice. How could we not follow her? Behind her magnetic words, the holier-than-thou declaimers of Astolfi and the blasphemers, the virginal and the deflowered, agreed to join the strike. Even the holdouts showed their mettle: ignited with reactionary passion, they brandished their faith in the Church and their disgust with the popular cause like a banner. No one remained indifferent when Leonora spoke. In the classrooms where small, private dreams had nestled for years, a political conscience began to grow like a new flower.

Not only did she defy the school authorities (they expelled her at the end of the year, despite her excellent average): her father, whom she loved (and whom I secretly wished was my own father), the

14

brilliant Professor Ordaz, an old-school idealist, loquacious defender of public education and friend of writers, was a government official who therefore (and in other ways) betrayed the dreams of his constituency. To oppose a government plan was to defy her father. But I was the only one who knew that. The others saw whatever they saw: a tall adolescent with a gypsy's face. And perhaps they believed less in her words – acquired words that she effortlessly made her own – than in the uncompromising, vibrant voice that pronounced them.

So it was that Leonora became the architect of that unusual thing that was becoming apparent in the prep school of the wisterias. But the one who pulled the strings was Celina. In secret meetings with the few Communist youths at the school, she formulated policies that came (as we later learned) from a higher authority. We two were her allies in the field, her confidantes and friends. It wasn't for nothing that she taught us a secret, last stanza that we sang quietly, savouring the nectar of rebellion: and if Franco doesn't like the tricolour flag (rumbalabum-balabumbambá, ay, Carmela), we'll give him a red one with a hammer and sickle (ay, Carmela). But we didn't interfere in her decisions.

I can't say that being left out bothered me. I've already stated that early on – and not without some conflict – I had accepted the fact that politics wasn't my destiny. Besides, on the wall of my room I had a poster of Picasso's "Three Musicians," and in my soul was the melancholy of being "the grey beret and the peaceful heart." I loved the rustic nobility of Maciste the blacksmith and Raúl González Tuñón's verses; I was rocked in the cradle of Communism and didn't mind having decisions made for me.

Leonora, on the other hand, wasn't one to let herself be rocked. Shortly after that September, she told me she had a secret to share with me. It must have still been springtime because the memory of it blends with a certain perfume and with an almost painfully intense awareness of being alive.

She had slipped her arm around my shoulder and, as on so many other occasions, we started walking along Plaza Almagro. A habitual gesture, that embrace, clearly required by the four inches she had on

15

me and by a certain matriarchal attitude she always assumed. We both liked – or now I think we both liked – to walk like that, as though feeling the other's body made us strong enough to sustain the universal laws we invented right then and there as we walked along, which were designed to eradicate stupidity, injustice, and unhappiness from the earth. I was the lawmaker, quite adept at inventing theories for everything, though too shy or carried away to convince anyone who didn't know me as well as Leonora did; so it was she, not I, who was in charge of using those arguments whenever the time came.

But that afternoon there were no arguments or theories. There was a revelation that shook me. I've thought a lot about her decision that spring. Maybe I still think about it, and maybe that's the real reason I'm writing these words.

"I have to tell you a secret," Leonora said as we walked arm in arm. "I've joined the Communist Youth."

Her activism didn't change things between us, at least not until she met Fernando. We told each other more secrets, and on our graduation trip (in spite of her expulsion, everyone, even her enemies, wanted her to come along), we scandalized the other newly credentialed teachers, as one can see in the photos. But without a doubt, something seemed to change in Celina Blech, whose knowledge of Berkeley now dazzled me somewhat less. Leonora had loaned me Politzer's The Elementary Principles of Philosophy, and there they all were: Berkeley and Heraclitus and Locke and Aristotle and Descartes, fixing their positions definitively for or against the revolution.

I ran into Celina last year. She told me she had an important position in a multinational company – she's a chemical engineer – and that she was about to go to Canada to work. I can't stand this violence, she told me, and we talked about the violence of the Argentine Anti-Communist Association and about the madness that the rebel group, the Montoneros, was committing in their desperation. The worst part isn't the fear of death, she said; the worst part is that now I don't even know which side the bullet might hit me from. I asked her if she was still a Party member. She smiled condescendingly, like someone who *had long ago forgiven the girl she once was. She asked me about Leonora. I told her I didn't know where she was, and I wasn't lying. How could I know her whereabouts that threatening winter of 1975?*

◆

She's no longer thinking about trees. She's walking along Wenceslao Villafañe, heading towards Montes de Oca. This might seem baffling to a spectator following behind her: why take such a roundabout route to go a single block? What the spectator wouldn't understand is that, except for a deceptive interval containing an embrace that Diana Glass categorized as triumphant and belonging to the realm of hope, for some five years now the mere act of moving from one place to another has obliged her to undertake some disorienting manoeuvres. She knows – she is, or has been, a more than competent physicist – that in Euclidean terms, a straight line is the shortest distance between two points, but it isn't always the safest. And a leader, above all, must always have her own security in mind, as Diana thought five years earlier, beneath a dusty sky.

She's late because she couldn't risk waiting for me. The thought doesn't comfort Diana: for the last few minutes, she's done nothing but gaze towards Díaz Vélez and towards Cangallo with little spastic turns. A waste of time, useless, since it's unlikely she'll be able to recognize her from so far away, as she used to do at the time the tree fell on her head. Not only because on this July afternoon, she's much more nearsighted than she was that spring *(a surprisingly early spring, or so it seemed to me because never before – and never since – did I feel so intensely the fragrance of the wisterias at the Prep School or the pleasure of walking down the street bare-armed. Everything was happening for the first time that spring when I was fourteen. Life, I said to myself, is something formidable that knocks you over like a wave and which not everyone can feel in its total splendour. "The two of us, you understand, we really do know how to feel life, the transformation of life, in our own bodies." I* liked those words: *transformation, life, bodies; I loved words because they were capable of preserving each thing in its perfection. Leonora needed them less than I did because Leonora was her dark body, and she especially was her hair, long and coppery, heavily undulating to the rhythm of that body. And yet, during that spring of 1957, words and things were inseparable for me, as well. Wisteria was a melody and a perfume and a shade of blue, as if everything around me had conspired to make me happy)*, not only, as I say, because on this July day she's more nearsighted than she was that spring, but also because she can't even be very sure of recognizing her from a distance.

They've seen one another only three times in the last ten years, under precarious conditions: the first time, at the Ordaz home, among old pots and pans, dying of laughter at age nineteen because they understood – or cared – very little about such chores, but nostalgic in spite of their laughter, or at least Diana was nostalgic, watching, a bit mystified, as Leonora put together an outlandish trousseau because she was going to marry the most beautiful – and the purest, Diana would think one night at a party – militant Communist in the College of Sciences: Fernando Kosac, with his grey eyes and transparent gaze. They seemed like a lovely adolescent couple from some Russian film, she would think nine years later as she read the police reports in the paper. The second time was also at the Ordaz place – Fernando was on a trip, she explained without further clarification – when their daughter Violeta was born, and Leonora, always knowing her place in the world, was all bosom, milk, and opulence. The third time was during an encounter so fleeting that she didn't even have time to look at her friend carefully. Diana walked through the Ordazes' front door at the exact moment when Leonora was rushing out, so they bumped into each other. They exchanged a kiss, and Leonora, one second before shooting out the door, said, "They killed Vandor."

It was surprising, but not so much the death itself. At that time, history still seemed logical to Diana, as did death. And a traitor was a traitor. Stumbling unmethodically, history marched irrevocably forward. That's the way it was. Only she, always so speculative, didn't have the time or the desire to stop and think that "forward" was as perfectly opaque an expression as "yonder" or "in the olden days," capable of obscuring more than just history.

It was surprising because the tone didn't match the meaning. As if she really had said Violeta has a fever. They killed Vandor: that's why I have to leave in a hurry.

"We'll talk another day, when there's more time."

But there was no time. Because, as always, ever since their return from the trip to Mendoza, life carried them along divergent paths.

And so they hadn't met again since the day before that dusty afternoon, if you can call something that happened in the intersection of two incompatible dimensions a "meeting." Diana, lying in bed, reading the paper and drinking *mate*, and Leonora fleeing to who knows where, from an announcement on the police report page.

What the report said:

That a highly dangerous terrorist cell had been uncovered. That the boldness of its constituents was immeasurable. That the subversives had been planning to blow up the official booth on July 9, when the Argentine and Uruguayan presidents and their entire retinues would be watching the parade. That to that end they had planned to use a fuel truck they had stolen in Nueva Pompeya, loaded with ten thousand litres of gasoline.

The question that crossed Diana's mind (momentarily interrupting her reading): How do you steal a fuel truck? And this query generated what threatened to become an unending chain of thoughts, starting with the initial question: how do you steal a fuel truck? This chain led nowhere and was destined merely to chase its own tail, to spin meaninglessly around the woman lying in bed, thinking (*there's a sort of action that's totally alien to someone accustomed to thinking in bed while drinking* mate, she wrote, embarrassed or melancholic, that same afternoon on the back of a deposit slip) and indirectly wondering: Would I be capable of stealing one? And even more incisive: Do I have any right to speak of revolution, to want a revolution, when I can't even steal a fuel truck? This precipitated a conflict that threatened to degenerate into another, indirect question leading to unforeseeable conclusions, specifically: If I were certain that stealing the fuel truck would lead unfailingly to revolution, would I steal it? This, in turn, seemed to hide the corollary: it isn't certain that stealing the fuel truck would lead to revolution. Suddenly, a name, casually noticed on the newspaper page, yanked her abruptly from those Byzantine musings.

What was that name? Kosac.

What she did next: she turned back and read: *It all began at dawn on Wednesday, when police personnel armed with rifles raided an apartment at the intersection of Juan B. Justo and San Martín. The police managed to collect a large quantity of subversive data and materials that led to further measures being taken. The place was vacant, but neighbours informed this newspaper that it had been occupied by a young couple named Kosac and their approximately five-year-old daughter. These two subjects were among those individuals most actively sought by the police. "They were very friendly," affirmed a neighbour who refused to give her name. "Very nice; they always greeted me in the elevator."*

She didn't steal a fuel truck, but she did take action in her own way: got up, got dressed, grabbed a taxi, and fifteen minutes later was standing before the Ordazes. I'm here for whatever Leonora needs, brave little soldier raised on the Maid of Orléans and Tacuari's Drum. Which led her to receive an anonymous call the next day: My dad said you wanted to see me, and even before recognizing the caller's voice, she recognized the turn of phrase, crystallized in her childhood like a school snapshot.

For which reason she's been waiting for half an hour at the entrance of the school, looking first towards one corner and then another with a not altogether unwarranted fear, since something more suited to a morbid imagination than to the realm of possibilities was happening that winter of 1971. Not long before, a lawyer had disappeared, and just a few days earlier, they took away a young couple. The man's bullet-riddled body had been found in a ditch, but no one knew anything about the girl, and that was more terrible than the fear of torture or death; it was a black hole containing all possible horrors, something they hadn't been prepared for, she thought, referring to herself and Leonora one specific summer night, singing their hearts out by the river, as though the joy of being adolescents and the need to change the world and the heroic ballad of a defeat were one and the same thing (*Mother, don't stop me for even one minute / for my life's of no value if Franco is in it*), not realizing, or not realizing entirely, that they were beginning to become impassioned with death.

No, not impassioned: familiar (as the olive-skinned woman who was about to reach Montes de Oca might have corrected her). And once you become familiar with death, nothing is ever the same.

But the one who waited for her at the entrance of the school five years earlier wouldn't have understood her, since, even though she's beginning to fear death, she's hasn't yet passed through a time of death that the one about to turn onto Montes de Oca knows quite well, since she's seen death at close range, has planned deaths, and, with a firm hand and even firmer resolve, has killed a man.

The one who waits tries to forget about death. She thinks – has thought: she's late because a leader must think about her own safety above all; she couldn't risk waiting for me there. Which very feebly minimizes an unbearable idea: something has happened to Leonora, and another, even more miserable thought: the phone call was tapped; the man at the kiosk who hasn't taken his eyes off me for a while now is there to take us both away, and what if Leonora doesn't come? A thought that remains happily incomplete because in the distance, on Díaz Vélez, waving with her arm in the air just as she did during the spring of the fallen tree, Diana sees – or thinks she sees – that person who, now, five years later, with a haughty gait and a haphazard detour, is entering the same street she left ten minutes ago.

◆

Only this time the detour proves useless: in the first place because the house with the white door is empty, and in the second because no one is following her: they're waiting for her.

A certain breakdown in her contacts – something she paradoxically had noted in one of the two letters hidden in the false bottom of her purse – doesn't allow her to know the first fact. And for five years she's been accustomed to avoiding thinking about the possibility of the second: a warrior is obliged to take all precautions to avoid falling, as she teaches the novices; but once taken, she mustn't think about danger: that would only weaken her in battle. For that reason, she's concerned only about what she will say in the meeting of the Secretaries General. She knows it won't be easy to justify what she wrote in the letter. Not in the one where she mentions the lack of contacts, which is strictly a technical problem that doesn't require justification – the military government, carrying out kidnappings with impunity, is destroying the network of contacts, so that she cannot locate the Montonero presses in the capital, if, indeed, there are any left; in order to keep functioning as Press Liaison, she needs to make new connections in La Plata . . . (The prose is deplorable, Diana thinks, reading the back of a photo where Leonora appears by a window, radiant, rubbing her beatific eight-months-pregnant belly. *Dear Friend: This letter is to inform you . . .* What makes Leonora, a revolutionary from head to toe, write like an old Spanish teacher? She decides to omit the transcription of letters and

dedications from her story; it would give the wrong impression.)
It's justifying the other letter that's going to be difficult. And not
because there haven't been enough resignations in her life – from
the Party to join the splinter group, from the splinter group to join
the Revolutionary Armed Forces, from the Revolutionary Armed
Forces to join the Montoneros – but she always knew how to
make those resignations seem like a leap forward. This one, on
the other hand, doesn't seem a leap in any direction; it's not even
exactly a resignation, but rather the rejection of an offer. What to
call it?

(Existential problems, Fernando, the most implacable of the
four, would say, bourgeois scruples.

She wouldn't respond to the insult. With authority she
would point out that so many desperate deaths were hardly
political.

"They're killing us," Fernando might say. "Our response
must be to kill them."

Would she have the courage to say she didn't like any of it,
that the people were now rejecting them and she didn't like that?

"It's not a question of what you like," Fernando would say at
that point. "It's a matter of following strategy, and strategy is
decided at the Commander level" – pause, eloquent look – "and
by the Secretaries General." Without intending to, he would see
her as he had seen her for the first time, with her flaming hair and
her haughty expression, entering the College of Science, and
then he would resort to the only method he knew of swaying her.
"Accept the post of Secretary General we're offering you, and
then you can discuss strategies with us. As an equal.")

What would she reply to that? For the moment, she doesn't
care: she's confident of finding the right response when the time
comes. She's not used to losing, and an unwary observer watching
her walk along Montes de Oca would agree.

But the five men observing her are not unwary: they've
been waiting for her for a half-hour, two of them from inside a

car on the corner of Wenceslao Villafañe, and three others a few yards away, pretending to chat on the sidewalk. And it's likely that at least four of them haven't acquired the habit of reflecting on something like this: the rhythm of a gait can encode the secret of a man or a woman. *One must love life*, Diana will jot down days after this event, as the Bechofen woman observes her from another table, thinking: she has too much passion to give shape to what she's writing. And yet, isn't that where the seed of all creativity lies, in passion? *One must revere life in order to form even an inkling of how much is sacred within a woman walking down the street.*

Those four seem only to spy a possible prey that the fifth man, sitting next to the driver, hasn't even noticed yet. Perhaps, against his will, he's dazzled by the *élan vital* emanating from the woman who has burst into view on Montes de Oca. Or maybe a certain thread, about to break, still links him to that man who, intoxicated with the spirit of the times, once said that it was necessary to join the struggle, to become the struggle in the name of the dignity of the people. *Who knows?* (Diana Glass will ask herself one day). *Who knows at what moment or under what circumstances a man becomes a life-hater? Or is he born that way?* And she'll ask herself this question, turning herself inside out to see if she can discover in herself how a chain of events, a singular combination of received words, can sculpt one in a unique, immutable way. *Or is it that a saviour or a criminal or a traitor nests within each of us, just waiting for the right opportunity to leap out?*

The man in the passenger seat still hasn't made a move: he's facing a new situation, and this, naturally, slows his action. It's not that he's the type to hesitate: two days before, he had no problem telling the Chief of Intelligence, known as the Falcon: "The meeting is going to be in a house with a white door on Montes de Oca and Wenceslao Villafañe." But to point out a woman who, like the Pasionaria, addressed students at university assemblies – she was addressing him, an implacable and enthusiastic science student – to move his mouth or his hand and communicate, "That's the one," is something else entirely. He's watching the woman walk along, confident, jaunty, self-assured, unaware that in a few seconds she will be subdued. And that power seduces him, but it also paralyzes him. For that reason he doesn't speak: it's the man sitting at the wheel who says:

"Is that the one?"

He just nods. Then he leans his head back against the headrest. It was easier than he thought: he simply let himself be, ceded gently in the name of life itself, barely confirming something that someone else like him would have confirmed sooner or later. He or someone else, what difference did it make? He closes his eyes for a moment, so that he doesn't see the signal the man at the wheel makes to the ones waiting on the sidewalk. Nor does he see – someone has removed him from the car in order to carry out the task from a different place – how those men advance and, so swiftly that a pedestrian on sun-filled Montes de Oca Street couldn't (or wouldn't want to) tell if this was happening in the real world or in a dream, force the olive-skinned woman's arms behind her back.

The Thrush, thinks the woman, who knows the Thrush's propensity for sick jokes. She feels fleetingly protected by that joke, as if by a bell that protects her in some ancient territory of camaraderie, so much so that she admits what she never would have otherwise admitted: that, in spite of her haughty gait, now that so many others around her are falling, in a certain part of her heart she feels afraid. Because she truly and intensely loves life. Even though there is no unwary observer of this scene to note that the hooded woman shouting, "They're taking me away!" and yelling out a telephone number that no one remembers was born to drink life down to the bottom of the glass.

Two

The story is continuously revised; it becomes hopeful or adventurous or tragic. That's why, right now, surrounded by worn photographs and moved by an overwhelming but uncharted impulse, she yearns for (among other things) the state of grace or of faith she felt that afternoon at Café Tiziano when, for the – second? – time, she thought about telling a story. Which wasn't yet exactly the same one she developed later on. Much less this one.

Perhaps she wove her story in order to lessen the fear instilled in her by waiting in uncertain cafés (ever since the meeting at the school entrance, she'd been engaging in a slightly clandestine activity: exchanging envelopes between Leonora and the Ordazes, envelopes whose contents she is unaware of, picked up at some café whose location Leonora had surreptitiously revealed to her over the phone: "We'll meet at four; two blocks south of where the art professor used to live"; a pale act of militancy that doesn't prevent her from not knowing which way is south, although some purely aesthetic sensibility kept her from sullying those mysteries with mundane interruptions like: "Just tell me the address of the café." "Even though it was just an aesthetic sensibility, my child," the Bechofen woman would say in that vaguely Germanic tone of voice that protected and slightly mocked her at the same time, "maybe you avoided questions like that because you couldn't accept the fact that even some 'revolutionaries' harbour formality in their hearts." Therefore it wasn't unlikely that she might be waiting in the wrong place, which produced a fear unlike the fear of death, but which didn't hide her fear of death, although it's also possible that she spun the story for a less readily admitted motive: the compelling need to justify somehow her reason for being there, or more precisely, to justify somehow her own existence in relation to someone else who justified her own existence all by herself. *Because action* (as she would jot down on the back of a receipt) *or rather, putting one's own body into action, means unconditional self-justification.* In order to quiet her conscience, which was more troublesome than her fear, she had to demonstrate – even more than believe – that their mutual destiny was to build a world that, on that afternoon and all that season and for two years afterward, seemed to be within arm's reach. The point was to see how each one of them would place her little tile. (In her version, the story was optimistic.) In fact, after waiting at Café Tiziano for twenty-five minutes (Leonora was still late), she thought it would be illuminating to write something that might resemble (as the shadow of a thing resembles that thing) the story of the two of them.

Strictly speaking, it was about two friends who began forming a common destiny at a very poor elementary school in the Almagro District. Two girls with restless minds, quick at math, rather badly behaved and avid consumers of all those books written for boys – or even girls – of their generation. This last fact was very important, since it was a matter of seeing how certain texts forged a revolutionary spirit in certain individuals who had been born in the forties. That was the heart of the artichoke: to respond to a few questions swiftly crossing her mind as she sat, ignited, at a table at Café Tiziano: How is a revolutionary created? What experiences, what unique sensibility for living those experiences, makes some people want to change the world? And, on a more intimate level, why, taking as a point of departure two girls of comparable intelligence and similar experiences, does one become an activist and the other an intellectual?

The notion was fairly complex since, while she needed only to consider Leonora in her present role (albeit slightly idealized), in order for the story to have some consistency, she needed to think of herself as having accomplished what at that moment she imagined she could – or must – accomplish. Hazily, impetuously, she realized whatever she wrote would have to be a conflation of the day when Leonora, slipping her arm around her shoulder, said she had a secret to tell her and the strange music (a mixture of cans and measured lumbering) of the milkman's wagon. Everything that contributed to her era and the formidable changes that affected the times in which the two of them were destined to live.

The strange thing is that when she considered how to begin, without any premeditation, and permanently adding a touch of whimsy to her story, she took one of Café Tiziano's paper napkins and wrote: *One splendid, sunny spring morning in my fourteenth year, a tree fell on my head.*

◆

Now she is only this blind body. The rough surface of a wall, the virtual construction of a dialogue, some splotches of sunlight on her face, something that just a few seconds ago had outlined the diverse accident of life has been reduced to the weight of six shoes stepping on her flesh and an abrupt absence of apprehension: she no longer has to think about how to justify her decision to the others. Instead of apprehension, there is nothing. Just the weight of some shoes and this perfect state of motionlessness.

And yet some nostalgia for her previous state must be fluttering within her because the combination of two phenomena puts her on guard. The cry "Bystanders at port," detected among several "Affirmatives" and "Commie bitch" and the sensation that, for a few seconds, the darkness surrounding her has no cracks in it. It was a brief, insignificant disturbance, however; beneath the blinding hood, she has put a seemingly preordained mechanism into motion. The fragile warp of light filtering once again through the hood reassures her that the sun has briefly disappeared. In the abstract, it's a simple problem: a length of sunlight, a portion of shadow, a length of sunlight. What they've just gone through must be a tunnel. And she clearly heard the word "port." So she knows where they're taking her: she has fallen into the hands of the Navy.

"Watch what you're doing . . ."

Her voice, accustomed to eloquence and command, seems able to create a certain suspense, even through the hood: their silence indicates that they're waiting for the end of the warning.

". . . because you're going to have to explain this mistake to my cousin . . ."

. . . the Captain, that's what Leonora called him, as I died of desire. I think he was a second cousin or something like that, and he adored her. It's hard to reconstruct that feeling now; I'd have to rub off a patina of fear, stepping over the rubble of bombings and lacerated bodies, plunge into the depths of memory in order to recall that in those days the word sailor *made you think transparently of the sea, the inexhaustible adventure contained in the word* sea, *boats tossing about in a storm, pirates commandeering a ship with daggers between their teeth, waves like gigantic beasts, an infinite blue. And the word* Captain . . . *oh Captain, tall and straight at the helm, peering at the horizon:*

> *Sail on, my noble ship,*
> *Sail dauntlessly,*
> *Your path unhindered through the sea*
> *By storm or calm or enemy . . .*

Pirates, the roaring music of the sea, bravery and freedom could all be summed up in the word "Captain." I had never seen My Cousin the

Captain, but I imagined him as a solitary, tanned man with eyes as blue as the dream of the sea, with one foot on the prow of his ship, crossing the ocean. He brought her gifts from all his voyages. I remember a box of plastic utensils (in those days it was called "plastic material" and was a delightful, much-desired substance), its cover like a tiny Venetian blind, with sections labelled in English. But what I remember most is the building set he brought her from England. Sitting at the hall table, listening to Tarzan, we constructed houses, forts, and pagodas with the amazing, hollow little wooden bars brought from England by My Cousin . . .

". . . Rear Admiral Mandayo."

The words float in the silence of the car advancing towards its destination. Has some bit of information been pronounced very quietly over the two-way radio? The fact is, until the car stops, no one calls her "Commie bitch" again or warns her of what in a few minutes they will do to her vagina.

◆

But there was a night when she found a different beginning and, for the only time, thought she had the ending. It was around the time a poet wrote: *The people who return, swearing merrily / retracing their moons of humiliation / swallow disadvantage and death / snatch slogans from the gutters / and emblazon them across the sky,* and she herself jotted down in an old receipt book that it was beautiful, after so many clandestine appointments, to see her walking along Corrientes as though the street belonged to her. *And it is hers, really. It belongs to all of us, at last.* They liberated the political presses, speakers talk about the Socialist Fatherland on the radio, and the people shout: Ay, ay, ay / Wouldn't it be swell / to build a Children's Hospital / in the Sheraton Hotel. It's true, for the moment, that the Sheraton is occupied by the same old Yankee tourists. They come to observe us, but what do they find? The people who return, swearing merrily and retracing their moons of humiliation.

And so it was the night of a time of happiness. To be more precise, the crisp, chilly night of June 11, 1973. Diana was walking absent-mindedly along Corrientes when someone came running up behind her and covered her eyes with their hands. She touched those hands, especially noting the palms against her face, as unmistakable and gentle as if they had no bones and could lovingly drape over the topography of a face.

"Leonora," she said, like a prayer.

Then, like someone who has heard the correct answer, the other person let go.

It was the embrace of two people who have just returned from a long war to discover that the other one has also survived. Much later, at home and drunk with happiness, she told herself it was like a dream that she and Leonora could have embraced like that out in the open, without the fear of death. And she thought she knew then what she wanted to write.

What she wanted to write was a sort of parable that would begin that miserable afternoon when she waited at the entrance of the school beneath a dusty sky and would end with this triumphant embrace, in a realm of hope. Subtly she would explore the large and small facts in the past that had made this embrace possible. Without the need to be explicit, it would be obvious that both political and intellectual support were essential for that nascent world.

Two obstacles arose: the first of a formal nature. No sooner had she begun to delve into the details of that wait beneath the dusty sky, right at the moment when the waiting woman thinks she spies the awaited one waving to her from Díaz Vélez, she intuited that in order to create a reasonably faithful version of the facts, she needed to mention something that would hobble the story from its very inception. She was vacillating over this when the second obstacle arose: Perón came, spoke of Argentine power, released his Peronist Youth and his passionate soldiers into the Plaza de Mayo, and life began to plummet quietly into despair. And so, what for a few days had been a happy ending became a dream-like memory: a slender, olive-skinned woman who embraces her in the night with the same passion and joy with which she had embraced her during the summer of the tree.

◆

"We know exactly who you are."

The voice, directly before her at the level of her head, was coldly polite. The prisoner (who lacks the habit of letting things pass) asks: "Who am I?"

And thus the reply of the one standing before her now could be construed, in a way, as an obligatory response, an act of obedience. The voice doesn't waver. Impersonally, it replies.

It startles her to hear her real name. Not because it's dangerous; quite the contrary, that name refers to a highly regarded scientist who existed up until five years ago, the young cousin of Rear Admiral Mandayo, and (why not?) her father's daughter. Didn't he tell her himself, without concealing a twinge of pride – *the pride with which he pronounced "educate the sovereign," making me dream that the man was my father* – that the Admiral into whose trap she has fallen is interested in certain political projects that affect him and his cohorts? It startles her because for five years she hasn't been the person designated by that name: she's the one designated by her *nom de guerre*. She's the one who is loved by her comrades and admired by the novices she has instructed; she's the one who has written inflammatory articles and planned precise operations and directed the implacable Organization newspaper. Even for Fernando (who also has a different real name), she is the one denoted by that name. Except in secret meetings with her parents or in some other ghostly meeting that she has tried to relegate to ancient, dead time (*I remind her of the summer of the turquoise skirt and she looks at me as though she never belonged to that world, or as though she were thinking when will she knock off all this pointless nostalgia? so I can give her these papers for my father and get on with real life)*; except during those furtive path-crossings, nobody has ever pronounced her real name again. (Just a few hours later, as she lies naked and chained, as they stick the electric cattle prod into her vagina, they will tell her – perhaps for the simple purpose of softening her up – who revealed her name and pointed her out on Calle Montes de Oca. "We picked him up three days ago and he spilled everything," they'll tell her. The prisoner will understand: the guy was a student at the College of Science, and at a clandestine assembly, days after the night of the long sticks, he shouted out that he was fed up with so much armchair Communism, and he shouted, "Viva Perón, goddammit!", and she, presiding over the assembly, barely nodded at him without revealing that she had some reservations about his Viva Perón. That guy had a reason to know her name: he knew her from another time. But she wouldn't understand this until a few hours later, with the cattle prod in her vagina.) Now she merely suspects that her real name might be an advantage.

"I know something else you can't imagine," she says.

And she vaguely suspects she'll be able to manage the situation.

◆

In fact the story of the two of them – if indeed there's anything that might be called a story-of-two, she thinks perversely, immediately cancelling the objection with a close look at a school photograph – began twenty-one years before the dusty afternoon, one April morning that Diana Glass had anticipated with dread the entire previous summer. It was her first day of school; however, through a double accident, she didn't begin at the beginning: through sheer inquisitiveness, she had learned her letters and a few numerical relationships on her own, and through sheer cowardice, she didn't have the courage to mention – she thought it annoying to confess things like that – that she was terrified to start off with the stigma of being different from the others in that unknown grade two class. She was inquisitive, but, no doubt, she couldn't anticipate all the possibilities. An unanticipated problem was occurring before her eyes: the grey-haired woman had just written a sentence on the board whose meaning eluded her completely: *1950, the Year of the Liberator General José de San Martín*. What's a Liberator General? She thought: general cleaning is when you clean everything; so general liberating must be . . . She was relieved. There were those who liberated a little and there were those who went around liberating everything. She'd have time later that night to think about what this business of liberating was. Now a previously unknown fact intrigued her: years belong to someone. Could this be a bit of knowledge that only those who had completed the grade one were privy to? And would she ever have her own year? The year of Something-or-Other General Diana Glass, and another requirement of future prowess disturbed her: the students had to write that sentence *every day* (said the grey-haired teacher) in their notebooks, and they had to do it *before anything else*. Why? The grey-haired teacher's tone suggested that any omission or even alteration of this order constituted an irreparable crime. What would happen the day she forgot to do it, the fatal morning she scribbled even a tiny, innocent scribble *before* writing the ordained words? This danger, resounding into the depths of hell, was tormenting her when the real horror erupted.

The honey-voiced, grey-haired one said: "Nearly all of you know each other from last year," and Diana Glass thought: Have mercy, Lord, since she was a precocious, voracious radio fan, and obviously more of an orator than a Jew. But the entreaty, perhaps on account of its purely rhetorical nature, had no effect. The grey-haired one, with a cruelty found only in nightmares, ordered the students who hadn't taken the first term of grade one with Señorita Isidora to stand up.

This couldn't be happening in the real world, Diana thought: to stand among these seated strangers who had been in grade one with Señorita Isidora and who surely wrote every morning, before anything else: *1950: Year of the Liberator General José de San Martín*, without feeling a hole in the pit of their stomach.

Miserable, she stood up. The awareness of movement behind her made her turn her head.

It was such a quick turn that, in the ensuing years, she thought it unlikely that she had captured the image in as much detail as she would later recall, and she wondered if she hadn't embellished it over time. But now the image appears in that form, and, turning her head swiftly, she notices a tall, slender girl with dark skin and a gypsy face, her long, copper-coloured braids still bobbling. And that voice. She will not forget that voice. As she faces forward once more, wondering how she's going to explain her situation when the time comes, the voice, firm and just a bit too loud, reaches her from behind. It says, without anyone's having asked, that she wasn't in grade one with Señorita Isidora last year because her mama enrolled her too late. And Diana, who is standing next to the bench and still hasn't managed to assemble her own complicated explanation, dreams of being a tall, dark-skinned girl with as simple an answer as that and with those braids. She remembers this, looking at the photo in the thick silence of the night at the exact moment when two men replace the prisoner's hood and, grabbing her by both arms, lift her from the chair where she's been sitting and conversing with the man they call the Falcon, and carry her body, blinded once more, to the torture chamber.

Three

Para bailar la bamba se necesita una poca de gracia. The radio masks the screams. Or maybe no one is screaming now: the howls of the woman who was cursing began to fade before the music started, and the man hasn't been heard from for a while now. The man didn't curse: he just emitted a hoarse, heart-wrenching moan that never seemed to end; maybe he's still cursing underneath the volume of the music. *Una poca de gracia y otra cosita, y arriba y arriba.* Now the song is her only contact with the outside, except for the barely distinguishable slice of artificial lighting she can see through her hood. It must be nearly midnight by now. Two or three men entered at some point, moved something, swore, and went out again. It seems like a bad joke: the *picana,* the electric cattle prod in here isn't working, although it might be just a trick to soften her up, letting her listen to the screams. Or letting her hear what the first guy said when he squealed. Especially hearing what the first guy yelled along with his inhuman bellowing right after they left her in here. *He's telling them things he doesn't even know,* she thought, and she squeezed her eyes shut beneath the hood even though that effort was really for another purpose: to avoid asking herself something she couldn't have answered: if she would be able to withstand the torture without naming names. That voice still haunts her, yielding, undone, completely detached from everything that once allowed him to say I love you, good morning papa, let us raise our flags in the name of the dignity of mankind. She doesn't know if the worst part was that accusing voice or the woman's useless insults. *There's always a way.* She doesn't think it, but it's as though the outline of a similar thought is calming her, helping her not to scream as she waits alone in the darkness. Her legs don't hurt, only where the cuffs restrain her ankles, but the pain in her arms, stretched straight up, is unbearable. *Arriba y arriba y arriba iré, yo no soy marinero.* Now footsteps approach: two or more have come back in.

"Did you enjoy your little recess, bitch?"

"No."

Her reply is neither hostile nor obsequious: simply informational. Perhaps they're taken aback by the normalcy of her tone because, as they loosen the chains around her feet and hands, they don't speak to her again.

They carry her like a dead weight to another place. There they strip her. They lay her on a sort of table. When they lift her arms, she makes an effort not to scream.

Having her legs brutally spread open isn't painful. Or else it's a new kind of pain. The pain of knowing with her entire body, for the first time on that irrevocable day – for the first time in her life – that they can break her. There's always a way? She suspects they've brought her to the place where the screaming woman was. *Yo no soy marinero, soy capitán.* In here the *picana* works.

◆

But in that spring of 1957, words and things were inseparable entities for me, too (Diana Glass has just discovered, writes, in the middle of the night in a yellow-paged notebook, surrounded by photographs and abridged notes on the back of printed papers, as if the embers of the blazing bougainvillea have at last ignited a forbidden corner of her memory or of her will to create memory.) *I let myself get drunk on the heady perfume of the wisteria; I glanced towards the sky on any arbitrary night and the moon was an enormous ring of light, as though everything around me were conspiring to make me happy.* And now, effortlessly, without the intrusion of a sarcastic thought, as though for the first time in three years she knows what she wants to do, she begins reconstructing the key to that time, *an unsullied time,* she writes, *when life and thought and even her own conflicted body seemed to be in harmony.* Swept away by her words, she believes she's also talking about Leonora and her entire generation, *those of us who climbed into the last horse-drawn buggy and listened to the tinny music of the milkman's wagon and entered the age of questions while the muted echoes of the bomb could still be heard. (What's an atom bomb, papa? It's a little bomb, small like this, and they throw it down from above and kill people; and I imagine a man opening a sort of peephole in the sky and throwing a lighted lantern through it.) Those of us who drew incomprehensible charts of the Second Five-Year Plan on notebook paper, dressed in white school smocks but denuded of skepticism, reciting:* On this twenty-fifth of May / I want to say once more / that being Argentine / I am most thankful for / Born in this silvery land / where bread and work are sweet / where all men greet like brothers / wherever they may meet, *those of us who danced at the movies to "Rock Around the Clock" and sang "The Army of the Ebro" spiritedly (and somewhat belatedly) and read* The Communist Manifesto *passionately (and precociously) and truly had our whole lives before us and the revolution in our hands and believed we were at the threshold of everything, and one night, without prior warning, we fell into this fear as into a bottomless well.* And without prior warning, she falls, her words fall into the bottomless well of knowing with her entire body, as she desperately writes, that yesterday they broke into the house of some distant cousins and took everyone away, from the Jewish grandma to the teenaged grandchildren, knowing that she will feel a chill on the back of her neck every time she opens the door to her house, that the bells will no longer toll for Mike, the drunken giant, who went out early one morning to buy throat lozenges and was sent home four days later in a box, killed in a confrontation the police said, but what kind of confrontation could Mike the Giant be involved in? Diana imagines him, good-natured and drunk, saying to the night patrol, "Night, man," or "Chilly night, huh?" and bang-bang-bang, here he is, we've sent him home to you, killed in a confrontation. *In order not to think about this, this insanity and this emptiness, this suspicion that the world has gone mad in an awful way*, she writes, pausing like someone who has awakened without knowing how she's gotten to the very brink when what she wanted to do was talk about that unique, inaugural spring when, like a burning rose, life began.

◆

Water is for guppies. The man moaning in the shadows, emitting shrieks that don't seem human – or that shouldn't be heard by human ears – has probably drunk water. It's not hard to imagine it, his devastated anus, his useless genitals, his lacerated tongue, drinking avidly, as in a dream that fleetingly restores him to his forgotten human condition. No one has explained to him that during the application of an electric cattle prod it isn't advisable to drink, even if one's mouth is twisted with thirst, since water is a good conductor of electricity: the jolt will be intensified and he will let out a piercing shriek that will make the woman, lying naked and chained in the place where the cursing woman was before her, squeeze her eyes shut and think (now that she can think because the one who has brutalized her vulva, her nipples, and her gums is giving her a break, offering her water): water is for guppies.

The knowledge that the howling man has acquired in his fifty-three years of life is of a different nature. He has read Malatesta and Count Kropotkin and has fervently believed in freedom and solidarity; that's why he was proud that the students could find those beautiful liberal-minded books in his subway newspaper kiosk in the station by the university, books that had formed him and which would prepare those youths for the blowing winds of revolution. He loved to say "youths" and "winds of revolution." He's been a bit naïve and a bit melodramatic. Typical guppy, a water-drinker. Those are the first to fall, thinks the woman who lies naked, having just refused a glass of water.

The light blinds her: someone has lifted her hood. When her eyes grow accustomed to the light, she sees a very young woman with painted lips. She's flanked by two men, but not handcuffed (only when she finishes saying what she has to say and turns to leave does the woman who lies naked notice that one of her ankles is chained to a cannonball).

◆

It may have lasted until summer, she stubbornly thinks, in order to avoid hearing the siren that pierces the night like a wound, determined, in spite of everything, to resurrect the brief time when Leonora, tall and olive-skinned, and she, with her persistent, childlike demeanour, formed a perfect whole. Persistent childlike demeanour? she thinks, curiously, feeling the uncomfortable sensation of the passage of the years. Because that defining demeanour is now barely a vestige, a bruise, whenever a spontaneous burst of joy, highly inappropriate to her age and to Argentine history (this very afternoon, the bougainvillea), lodges in her body and makes her go a little wild. But only sometimes. Since there have been romantic whirlwinds and unnoticeable failures, including perhaps this very story that she insists on telling in order to find redemption or to erase the panic of the present moment – where are you, Leonora, on this moonless night, where are you escaping to, and how can you escape when even mothers and sweethearts fall? – generic and personal stories that have ravaged her face, so the word "childlike" would be imprudent. So she writes that all the happiness in the world was summed up in that spring: until the end of summer, she wore a blue pleated skirt and a sailor blouse, and Leonora wore a white shirt and the turquoise skirt – everything was turquoise that season – a detail that allowed Diana, despite her nearsightedness, to recognize her from afar the morning when she burst into the street because the intoxication of being alive overflowed the walls of her house.

First it was the skirt, like a big, patchy wave. Then the way she walked, and especially the way she waved from afar with her arm high in the air. Diana waved in return. Then they ran towards each other with that virile exuberance they were so proud of and embraced as if they hadn't seen each other in years or as if the meeting were taking place on a barren planet where they were the only survivors. "I came to meet you," "I was sure I'd find you," they said at the same time, and it was enough to make them burst into uncontrollable laughter, leaning into each other to keep from losing their balance. They embraced as they walked along, Leonora's protective arm around her shoulders, and her arm around Leonora's waist, drinking her in through her skin, as though they, the morning light, and the fragrance of the geraniums were a single, perfect, blissful body.

They walked along Salguero, discussing *Jean-Christophe,* whose passionate life both of them were reading; they talked about the fifteenth birthday party they would both attend that Saturday, about Leonora's boyfriend ("something really terrible is happening to him that I can't even tell you about," squeezing her shoulder to gain more strength), about a boy with glasses with whom Diana secretly was in love; of how they, just like Anne Frank, believed that people were really good at heart. They bought caramel apples in the plaza, sat down on a bench facing the Church of Guadalupe, and Leonora confided part of her secret: she told her (with omissions) of her boyfriend's tragedy, which was also her own. "His lifelong dream is to get into the Police Academy, but there's something very private that's keeping him out: something I can't tell anyone, not even you." Diana briefly wondered if it could be some character flaw or some horrible prejudice that kept *her* from having a hypothetical boyfriend with that ambition. Less briefly, she wondered what the private impediment could be: against her will, she located it in the young man's dick but didn't say anything, since, ever the aesthete, she loved perfect moments: no inconvenient observation must disturb that morning in bloom. Was our sacred morning, then, made of what I obstinately removed from the picture? Not now, please, now that I have the two girls sitting opposite the Church of Guadalupe in that blue moment forged by happiness, now that I'm discovering why I wanted to describe that morning and show the two holding hands and watching the changing patterns of sunlight on the church, don't let any evil thought come along and interrupt me. Cross out the business about the Police Academy, and for symmetry, eliminate the part about her thwarted love affair. Simply write that something is making Leonora unhappy. Then Diana pulls out a piece of graph paper, saying: "I'm going to read you a poem by Alfonsina Storni." She reads a love poem of which some verses sound like Storni and others like Héctor Gagliardi. "It's so beautiful," Leonora says. Diana confesses, "I wrote it myself." They embrace, overcome with emotion, and walk back down Salguero embracing, speaking of the miracle of life that they know better than anyone, and of all the noble things they feel capable of doing. And for the first time, ignoring the sirens and illuminated by her desk lamp's 75-watt bulb, Diana feels she has reached something, the end of the beginning, she thinks, a moment of supreme hope or supreme beauty from which all paths radiate to change the world, *because that lightning bolt of happiness, that painfully lovely realization that it* is *possible for people to be happy, was a short time later the very thing would lead us to the desire and the will to . . .* But perversely, as if her unbridled enthusiasm can no longer contain the maelstrom of her thoughts, she writes: *And then, as we passed single file through a very narrow place, at that moment of perfect happiness, a tree fell on my head.*

◆

"It's better to talk right away; don't let them destroy you. They messed me up good at first, and for what? A few less teeth, that's all I've got to show for my heroism. One day I couldn't stand it anymore and told them everything I knew. It was useful to them – that's the important thing. I don't know if you realize I had the codes for the meetings. And, well, it was useful to them. I think they fell like flies. So what? They would have fallen anyway. Those who must fall, will fall, because if you don't talk, someone else will – that's their whole philosophy. Only the people at the top know how to escape. I know what I'm talking about; they tell me certain things. But the people at the top are saving their own skins; they don't give a thought to girls like me. It's better to co-operate with these guys; they're not bad, you've got to get to know them, like anyone else. They told me if I do everything they say, when my baby is born they might not take him away from me. I'm pregnant, did I tell you that? The doctor here found out about it, that guy who revives you when you pass out. I'm due in June and they promised that if I don't let them down, I'll be able to . . . well, I wouldn't be able to raise him in here, but if I don't let them down, they might even give him to my folks. They're not bad guys; once you become their friend, they're much more respectful than some of the guys I used to know. That's the way it is – just like with anyone, if you're useful to them, you're sure to survive. If not, they'll kill you right away. I was lucky, see? I'm useful to them in certain ways, like I told you. And in other ways, too. Don't even think about it anymore: whatever you have to tell them, say it quick. I know what I'm talking about," said the girl with painted lips.

Then she picked up the cannonball and walked away, flanked by the two men.

◆

"We'll have to take her to the hospital." The man's authoritative voice was the first thing to pull her from the void. Not to the hospital, no, she doesn't know if she said it or thought it, and she desperately willed her eyes open.

But now nothing was like before: during the rest of that extraordinary summer, she knew she might die. *It was the scythe of death in the middle of a savage river of happiness*, she wrote that same night in a notebook of lined paper. She was fourteen, and every event struck her as dazzling and unique, even that premature experience of death. And perhaps it's an exaggeration to call it a "premature experience of death" (in fact, the tree wasn't really a tree but rather a very thick branch), but excesses were her *raison d'être* in those days. And the truth is that she had experienced the branch on her head as though it had been a tree, and her fall like the unwanted embryo of her grasp of precariousness. If not, why then do I keep slipping into my own personal obsession, wonders Diana Glass at the very moment when the prisoner, naked and spread-eagled beneath the interrogation lamp, bellows like a quartered beast. A red-hot current from her vagina to her teeth.

"This will make you talk, Montonero bitch."

She looks at the face of the one who spoke (no one has bothered to replace her hood). Nose, mouth, eyes. It's the face of a man.

"I have no one to name," she says.

"We'll make sure you do."

Now, as slowly as a submerged body, the hand holding the cattle prod moves towards one of her nipples. (Or else the slow motion is a subjective impression: it's a well-known fact that there are some moments that come into such close focus that, analyzed logically, they seem to last longer than they really do.)

"Look in my purse!" the prisoner shouts desperately, as if shouting, "Stop that cattle prod!" Then she seems to recover some of her composure. "There are two letters in there with the proof you're looking for."

"Proof of what?"

The approach of the *picana* has been suspended. Action hangs by a thread.

"Proof that I've lost all my contacts. I have no one to name because I don't know where to find anyone."

The man holding the *picana* laughs.

"That's not enough, bitch. We don't even bother to check bullshit like that."

Has the *picana* advanced a few more centimetres towards her nipple, or is it another subjective impression? The prisoner doesn't close her eyes. In a neutral voice, she says: "There's another piece of information in the second letter. It will tell you a lot about me."

This isn't betrayal, she would say to herself if she were in the habit of reflecting; in any case, I'm just betraying myself. Is that bad? To appear naked in front of people who have no business seeing me naked? Bad for whom? I'm already naked in front of them; they touched my body, poked inside my vagina. What difference does it make if they get their hands on my doubts about some of the methods the Organization is using? It's not as though the letter mentions my desire to escape, my desire to erase the past. You don't discuss those things in a letter to the Commanders unless you want to be shot. But these guys might be able to read between the lines . . . The Falcon's no fool; if he discovers my doubts and if that encourages him, so much the better. It's his job, not mine. My job right now is not to name names, and I'm not.

("Because naming names isn't for everyone," the man they bring in a little later will say. At first the prisoner will be surprised to see him alive. Hernández the Chimp. He was an important official who was picked up a month earlier; everyone on the outside had given him up for dead. He played the guitar like an angel. "To say a name and know that in a few hours the guy with that name is going to be begging to die on the torture table . . . it's not for people like us, and some of them know it. There are some intelligent guys among them, with the ability to get to know us. Know something? There are intelligent guys everywhere, that's what we didn't realize. And, well, if they give you a chance to let them know you . . . Do whatever you think best, but I'm alive; I don't know if this is a recommendation, but maybe it'll help you. I'm sorry if I can't give you more reassurance; that's not what they asked me to do. But it's the first time they've sent me to do something like this, and it turns out I'm talking to someone like you . . . . I hope I'm not misleading them," he will say, his hands trembling a bit, a slight breathiness in his voice, and the whole time he avoids looking at the spread legs of the woman who lies on the table, her body filthy with sweat and excrement, and her eyes . . . above all he avoids her eyes. Then, out of the corner of his eye, he glances at the man at his side, and in a slightly weary monotone, like someone who hopes to be understood without too much effort, he will add, his eyes fixed on the floor, that things can be different from what you might expect here, that if you can set aside certain principles, you might find a way to survive, technical jobs, nothing great, things you know how to do that are useful to them. He's sure, because he knows her, because he knows how talented and strong she is, that she'll be able to find her own way.

Then he'll pick up his cannonball, and, like the girl with painted lips, he'll walk out, leaving her alone.)

But all that will happen later. Now the prisoner is alone – the two men have gone looking for the letters – and although she doesn't reflect on it (she doesn't have that habit), she quickly decides that what she's doing isn't betrayal and that she's taken the right step.

She grows alert. Rapid footsteps are approaching. Two men.

"You lied to us, you little Montonero whore," the first one shouts as he walks in. "There was no letter in your purse."

She feels terrified, but only for a moment. She's just recognized the second man: it's the Falcon. *Yo no soy marinero*, she thinks, but addresses the other one.

"You've forgotten one detail," she tells him. "Don't you know that a purse can have more than one bottom?" Now she looks right at the Falcon. "You still have a lot to learn about us, Captain," she says.

The one who spoke is about to lean over her. "You little Montonero . . ." He doesn't manage to complete the phrase or the act. A gesture by the Falcon stops him cold.

"Go look for the letters where she said, Lieutenant," he orders, barely moving his lips.

Then he leaves, following the lieutenant. The prisoner remains alone, insofar as one can be alone. Her father isn't there, Fernando isn't there, the other men who loved her aren't there, the Party won't come to her rescue, and the top Montonero brass won't look out for her. To whom does she belong now? Who will protect her?

◆

Many times she would return at dawn, walking on tiptoe so as not to awake her mother who, if she heard her footsteps, might get up and yell in her face about what a disaster her life was; or her father, if he was at home, might come out to meet her and launch into one of his speeches about those useful idiots in the Communist Party (even though he wasn't right, his arguments were more convincing than Leonora's – and she couldn't reply, despite her fury, because she adored him). Leonora might have been returning from some street protest against the selling out of the oil industry, or from running off mimeographed copies of some flyer, or from a discussion with her comrades about what tactic to follow in the secondary schools "so the flame of battle won't be extinguished after defeat"; she would return tired and vibrant with revolutionary spirit but she had to go out of her way, always on tiptoe, in order to avoid her parents' bedroom door – behind which it wouldn't be unreasonable to imagine her mother, beautiful and alone, hearing the cautious footsteps and crying silently over her unfair destiny: a husband who was married to politics and this, her only child . . . oh, such a misfortune . . . . Then barely touching the floor, Leonora would cross the threshold of the little room where her angelic grandmother Violeta slept. At last she would enter her own bedroom, which, strictly speaking, wasn't her bedroom at all, since there, motionless in one of the twin beds, lay the living image of all that Leonora most detested in the world, her Aunt Adolfina, a bitter old maid, early riser and daily communicant of Our Lady of Mercy Church. "A candle-sucking old witch, Diana (Leonora said), a life-hater who every morning, afternoon and night recites the longest string of Our Fathers and Hail Marys that can fit in her head – the only thing that can fit in that head – as if that might redeem her from the poison she stores in her body." "Because she doesn't understand, Leonora (I said), that the only thing worth knowing about God is that we ourselves are God, the each one of us carries a God inside us. Isn't it true that everything good and beautiful that's possible in the world depends on you and on me and on everyone? That's why we'll be able to change the world. That's the only truth." And thus, arrogant and omnipotent and free as the wind, with this religious devotion, we expressed our independence of all gods, but especially of the bureaucratic God who only presided in churches and temples and mosques and to whom one had to recite empty, alien texts. That God invoked by the woman who lay waiting in one of the twin beds. And so the girl who had just come from painting walls or singing lovely Party songs around a campfire under the stars and who still trembled with revolutionary fervour, prayed somewhat fearfully as she undressed: Let her be asleep. But the plea to an addressee unknown was never heeded: scarcely had Leonora rested her head on the pillow, her body gently moulding itself into sleep than Aunt Adolfina's strident voice drilled through the stillness:

"Let's pray, Leonora. Let's say a prayer for all the lost souls wandering around the world and for God to forgive your sins." Then she, too weary to argue or to become enraged, pressed her palms together in the darkness, and, joining her voice to Aunt Adolfina's, meekly entoned: Hail Mary, Mother of God, pray for us sinners.

◆

Without a father, without a lover, without a Party. Alone to the extent that one can be alone while an unknown man reads a letter that one's life may depend on. And this time, without being able to count on the effectiveness of someone who has never failed her before: herself. Help me, dear God, the prisoner struggles to shout silently. Out of habit or pride she suffocates that cry. But foggily she perceives an order – the only one – that might yet help her in this darkness. Our Father who art in Heaven, she thinks forcefully, and a sort of peace, or hope, falls over her and quiets the frantic beating of her heart. Then, without pressing her palms together because her hands are chained, without kneeling because her legs are spread apart, alone within four bare walls, she lets her voice be heard, superimposed over military orders and distant moans. *Our Father who art in Heaven, hallowed be Thy name. Thy kingdom come, Thy will be done, on Earth as it is in Heaven. Give us this day our daily bread, and forgive us our trespasses as we forgive those who trespass against us. And lead us not into temptation, but deliver us from evil,* she recites, not missing a single word. *Amen.*

Four

Hair salons are protected places, secure areas where no one will throw you out for being an actual or potential disturbance, as they did six months earlier when the woman who is now thumbing absent-mindedly through a magazine before a large mirror was brutally fired from her job. No one is a disturbance in a hair salon. No person or thing can disturb them: safe and sound, they stand up to mobs and catastrophes; governed by their own set of rules and impregnated with their own special scent, they don't evoke the fragrance of wisteria or the unmistakable aroma of that pudding Grandma Violeta used to make every Christmas, so delicious that once you've tried it, it'll haunt you every Christmas for the rest of your life. Not even outside noises can get in. Or else they filter in so muffled by the interior hum, a mixture of voices and innocent machines, that they seem harmless. Not even death can infiltrate hair salons. You can simply relax while the stylist practices her honest trade and you can learn, reading old magazines, one hundred secrets to make him love you or twenty original ways to prepare cauliflower, or how to stay fresh and youthful while the outside world collapses in a chaos of muffled screams and broken bodies. Enough! We were saying that no conflict can filter into a hair salon. There must be some reason why the woman in front of the mirror has decided to come in and get a haircut.

She's just finished thumbing through the magazine with the cauliflower article and has picked up another one, a news magazine, luckily out of date. But not quite out of date enough, she observes, looking at a photo of an Argentine general smiling insincerely at a little boy. She turns that page, and the following ones, quickly, looking for a slaughterer, a girl with two heads, an unforgettable romance on golden sands, something to return her to that safe little world. She turns another page and sees, in bold black letters: **The Five Most Wanted Guerrilla Girls in Argentina**. She doesn't want to search for her among the five photos, but naturally she does. There she is, right in the middle, smiling, long-haired. Death doesn't neglect any openings: it's finally entered this pleasant hair salon, too. And Diana discovers why her story is chasing its own tail: it's she who stubbornly refuses to see the ending. But now that she knows it, there's no going back: she will go directly to the Ordazes' house and find out once and for all what has happened to Leonora.

"Do you like how it looks?" asks the stylist.

She keeps staring at the smiling face. She has the odd impression that, if she stops staring at it, that face will be erased forever.

◆

"Take off her hood."

She recognizes him without seeing him, by his voice and by his order. She's heard that order before – yesterday? the day before? – when she wasn't yet as she is now, spread-eagled and chained to the corners of a cot, but rather seated opposite a man whom, until just now, she had known only by voice.

"I know something you can't imagine," she had said, and the man facing her raised his eyes, trying to read through the hood.

"What do you know?"

"I know you're a marine and I know where I am."

She named the place. She calculated the impact it had on her interrogator by the slight change in tone of the questions that followed. She was trying to guess if they had already contacted her second cousin, Rear Admiral Mandayo, and if they had discovered who her father was, when a custom-made question, blasted out by her interrogator, made her put aside any further speculation.

"What kind of country do you people want?" the man facing her had asked.

The prisoner responded firmly, "We don't want Communism."

She hadn't lied; she was simply trying to organize her speech. When the man facing her challenged her about foreign ideas, alien to our national character, the prisoner spoke eloquently about national sovereignty, noting that the regrettable thing about this government – the only regrettable thing, she let slip as if by accident – was its Minister of Finance, a sellout to Yankee money. And so the man facing her had no alternative but to concur, although with some reservations. The prisoner countered some of those reservations while agreeing with others. If it hadn't been for the fact that one of the two protagonists had her face covered with a hood, the scene might have appeared to be a civilized exchange of views by two sharp-witted individuals. But this irregularity could be corrected. It happened when the man facing her, perhaps feeling uncomfortable at the direction the interrogation had taken, alluded to "you subversives with your promiscuity and atheism." The prisoner reacted haughtily to this.

"And you, who surely think of yourself as so righteous," she said to him, "do you think it's very macho to keep a hood on the woman you're speaking to?"

She knew something about the marines; in effect, there was a marine among their trainers in Tucumán; she knew through experience how proper they tend to be with women, different from those in the army or the police force. She recalled one after-noon when the marine instructor had gone too far ordering push-ups and she had scraped her knees. It's dishonourable! the marine had repeated, to the laughter of all her comrades; it was my fault a lady got hurt.

The man facing her couldn't tolerate having his virility impugned, either.

"Take off her hood!" he ordered.

And then, for the first time, she saw the Falcon's face.

Now she sees him for the third time, his cold, blue gaze studying her as it did at their first meeting. In that gaze, the pris-oner tries to discover how her letter was interpreted, but the Falcon's eyes reveal nothing. Whatever she knows, she knows because of two facts: she's alive, and in the two days she has been chained to this cot, no one has tortured her again. Besides, at some undefined moment, they've put her clothing back on her.

The Falcon looks her spread-eagled body up and down; then he turns to someone on his right. Just then the prisoner notices that he isn't alone: he's brought in a male prisoner. Dark hair, grim expression, cannonball. The Falcon orders: "Tell her what you have to say."

The male prisoner places the cannonball on the floor and begins speaking without looking at her, nothing very different from what the others have said, that the guerrilla movement is a lost cause, that he believed, too, at one time, that they were going to save the Fatherland but now he realizes how wrong he was, that the only thing they would have achieved, had they won, would have been to destroy Argentina irrevocably, and so the best thing for her, and for the Fatherland, would be to co-operate without hesitation. The marines are sensible people, more sensible than the other branches of the armed forces, and they have an interesting plan. A plan that might be of interest to someone like her.

The prisoner regards him for a few seconds. She's about to say something to him, but then, like someone who wishes to establish hierarchies clearly, she addresses the Falcon.

"This guy's not a prisoner," she says. "He's acting."

The Falcon observes her curiously, as if trying to capture something in her expression that escapes him.

"What makes you say that?" he asks.

"Because he doesn't have that scared look like the ones who came to see me yesterday and the day before." She fixes her gaze on the icy blue eyes studying her. "And he doesn't talk like one of us."

"And how do you people talk?"

She attempts a laugh. She has the feeling she hasn't laughed for ages. How strange all this is: spread open like a side of beef, she's still capable of formulating – she *is* formulating – a clever reply.

"For example, we never would have said 'Save the Fatherland.'" Her gaze, now, seems to come from far away, from a time when she was the one to make conditions. "There are lots of things about us you don't know, Captain."

Imperturbable, the Falcon turns halfway around. He looks at the man with the grim expression.

"Well, Sharkey, did you learn your lesson from the Montonera? That's what we need around here: intelligent people, people with balls."

Five

Seen from outside the Mecca Café, the older woman and the younger one present a kind of symmetry. Seated next to the only two windows in the café, each with pen or pencil in hand and a notebook or notepad on her table, they are positioned so that if they were to lift their heads simultaneously, their gazes would meet. It's happening right now. The younger woman has stopped staring out the window – she fleetingly glances straight ahead – and sighs dejectedly, and the older woman, who has just interrupted her writing and raised her head, smiles slightly in her direction as though she understands. As though she understands what? wonders the younger woman – not even I can explain what this means, this watching the front door instead of going right into the house, climbing up to the second floor, and asking have you heard anything from Leonora? as I used to do. What bothers her the most isn't her furtiveness but rather how naturally she accepts it, the ease with which she's been adapting to new little habits: waiting at this table instead of going into the house, or glancing every so often at the fox-eyed man who, ever since she arrived at the Mecca (she looks at her watch; it's been exactly one hour and forty-five minutes), hasn't moved from the corner. Just a coincidence? Or permanent surveillance of the house? Aside from this state of suspicion, there's nothing unusual. The man behind the counter chats pleasantly with a mustachioed guy eating a croissant; the waiter hums "Francisco Alegre," and the older woman who smiled at her a moment before is writing on her notepad without any external indication to suggest anything different from how it might have been ten, or twenty, or forty years ago. Forty years ago, I must have been like this girl, the older woman writes, and if not for my wrinkled skin, for a few brownish spots on the hand that's writing, nothing would tell me I'm any different. Or would it? That expectation with which she stares out the window, a certain skittishness, no longer define me, and I can't say I'm sorry. All I want is to have her story, to discover why she's staring out the window, what it is she saw just now that made her eyes grow wider. Aunt Adolfina, thinks the younger woman, wondering if the expression on Aunt Adolfina's face might reveal something about what she's trying to find out. It doesn't reveal anything because she never saw it except through Leonora's scornful eyes. Aunt Adolfina is crossing Medrano with a pensive expression, perhaps returning from the Church of La Merced, just as she did twenty, thirty years ago, as though nothing on earth had changed. And she herself, isn't she experiencing the same compulsion to jot things down, isn't she jotting things down right now in her yellow-leafed notebook (the only one she's brought along), just as she recalls doing ever since she became an adolescent? Certain questions, certain conundrums about the apparently quotidian. And the strange thing is that this game (because it's nothing more than a game) gives her the same pleasure and the same uneasiness as it did back then. Nothing about her seems to have changed, and yet, for two hours she's been in this café, waiting for the Professor to arrive or to leave, simply because she doesn't have the courage to do something as simple as . . . . Suddenly she raises her eyes from the notebook and looks out the window. She's seen something in the distance that has surely shaken her up, thinks the older woman, because she's left the notebook on the table and has rushed into the street, as though something or someone were escaping her grasp. The man who was behind the counter also rushes out, shouting "She left without paying!" and he gestures to someone who must be on the corner whom the older woman can't quite see. "Halt!" The older woman hears, an authoritative and unknown male voice coming from the corner. It's a military order, inescapable, which unleashes a flurry of movement on the street. Then, through the window she sees the man who was behind the counter, another man who looks like a fox, and the young woman. The young woman is pale and looks agitated; she's trying to explain something. She points insistently at the table by the window where she has just been sitting. The man-who-looks-like-a-fox pokes a finger at her chest and says something. The young woman opens her purse and takes out her papers; her hands are trembling slightly. The man-who-looks-like-a-fox studies them suspiciously. At last he returns them to her, apparently with a warning. The man from behind the counter and the young woman return to the café. She pays, trying to be pleasant; she has lost her opportunity to meet with the Professor, so she'll have to come back another time. This is what's changed, she thinks as she leaves: death lying in wait, floating over the minutiae of daily life. The older woman watches her leave, brimming with curiosity. To unravel the meaning of these trivial, apparently unhistorical, actions, which nonetheless intercept History, diverting its course in unforeseeable ways. I confess, now, at the threshold of my seventh decade, that this is the only thing that interests me. Fifteen feet below the street level where these events have occurred, the prisoner hears a howl that squeezes her throat shut.

◆

"But I don't know anything," the howling man says. "I don't know anyone – what do you want me to tell you?" The Shark's voice keeps insisting, unflappable. Another howl pierces the darkness, a howl without words: it's feral. He's going to spill it, the prisoner thinks; even though he knows nothing, he's going to spill it. He's a guppy, he doesn't understand that even spilling it won't save him – he's finished, no matter what he does. The problem with guppies is that they don't know what the military is like: you're either a general or a good little soldier – otherwise, you're screwed.

She doesn't want to hear what the howling (now weeping) man is saying. A name? The location of a house? The Shark says it's not enough. There's another scream and once again the sobbing voice, naming names. She doesn't want to hear it. She prays a guard will come along to distract her from this nightmare. Because there's only one thing she can stand less than these sobs: solitude.

The guards aren't bad sorts; you have to know how to treat them, the same as anyone else: a friendly remark or even a joke when they bring her food or the bedpan; everyone enjoys pleasantries when they're working. The prisoner is sure she's made a good impression on them: sometimes they even bring her something to read; at those times, they remove her hood and free one of her hands. When they bring her food, they free both her hands, but just for a little while. In any event, now that the restraints are looser than at the beginning, she's figured out how to slip her hands out when no one is watching. She's always been very good with her hands. *Strange hands, as though they had no bones. It was amazing to touch them, a mixture of fascination and revulsion, dexterous hands that could draw shaded vases and sophisticated letters and that could insinuate themselves into any opening, mould to any shape. They were tender, with astonishingly smooth palms; you felt you could squeeze them into oblivion. And yet they were resilient; they emerged from oppression unscathed, as though life, which furtively marked our destiny in all of our hands, hadn't left a single trace on those. That was the first thing I recognized that joyous night in June of 1973, right at the door of the old Medrano Cinema, when someone grabbed me from behind, covering my eyes. A game that brought back to me, intact,*

other moments of delightful uncertainty, when I knew that my captor
wouldn't let me go until I guessed who she was. I did what I had done
when I was ten: I felt her hands. And a single contact with that end-
lessly ductile material was enough for me to recognize their owner, just
as when I was ten. Leonora! I shouted, and it was a resurrection. We
embraced with the same passion, the same joy as when we were four-
teen; it seemed as though an entire world separated us from our last
meeting at Café Tiziano, when we had to speak in whispers and
Leonora had come from an alien, clandestine place and both of us
feared for our lives – or else I feared for both of us. Now the streets
belonged to us and the Sheraton, too, ay, ay, ay, wouldn't it be swell.
The time for singing had finally come. Leonora (she told me) was
working on a project for the University, and I had discovered the end of
my story at last, two young readers of Salgari, who, with the pen, the
sword, and the word, and later by living through certain vicissitudes,
arrive at this triumphal night. A happy ending, under the stars, clap,
clap, clap . . . . And so, when there are no witnesses, the prisoner
can manoeuvre her hands nimbly, like putty, slipping out of the
handcuffs. It's nothing more than this, a small exercise in freedom, to liberate her hands, lift the hood a little if indeed she's
wearing it, touch her perspiring face, feel her filthy body, study
the movement of her fingers, a game that can free her momentarily from what she hates most: solitude.

Now she's alert because, despite various howls and the
noise of the radio, she thinks she hears steps approaching. Very
carefully, a hand removes her hood. It isn't a guard: it's the
Shark.

He's been coming every day now to ask her questions from
the same place where he had tried to pass himself off as a prisoner, that first time.

"You've been crying," he says this time.

"I never cry," the prisoner says.

"No, you never cry," says the Shark. "It's strange. But today
your eyes look red. Something's upsetting you today."

"What day is it?" the prisoner asks.

"October 18. You see? Your eyes are filled with tears again. You can't fool me."

"Today's my daughter's birthday," the prisoner says.

The Shark seems to hesitate.

"Your daughter. Ah. You should tell me about your daughter. How old is she?"

"Ten."

"And what sort of things does she like?"

"I don't know. Stories, sleeping all curled up like a cat."

"Does she like French fries?"

"French fries? Yes, of course, french fries. She likes them. She likes them a lot."

"Does she look like you?"

The prisoner regards him for a minute silently.

She's a perfect combination of them both: Leonora's olive skin, also her thick eyebrows and full lips, made for smiling, but her eyes are Fernando's: grey, transparent eyes. And her blonde hair, too.

"Yes," she says, "she looks like me."

The Shark stares at her oddly: he seems lost, as if something inside him has been misplaced. Suddenly he shouts.

"How could you?" he shouts. "How could someone like you have done it?"

"How could I have done what?" the prisoner says. She appears alarmed.

"Live with that Communist pig." For the first time he's looking at her with hatred. "You yourself," he shouts, pointing his finger at her, "you yourself are a Communist with no country and no religion."

She shakes her head from side to side.

"You have the wrong idea about me," she says. "I never stopped praying."

◆

She seemed unshakable; that's why it made such an impression on me the first time I saw her crying – the reason for her crying – and it even struck me as natural, later on, that she had found a way to staunch those tears, a way to charm Miss Tortosa. Miss Tortosa was our home economics teacher: skinny and pale as a ghost, with dyed black hair piled up in banana curls; a widow (which added a slightly murderous touch to her image) with a daughter our age who went to Catholic school. Every so often Miss Tortosa brought her to show her off, all lace and a white bow, the perfect picture of what Leonora and I most detested in this world. Miss Tortosa always wore black; she had a hook nose and nails like claws, polished scarlet. She looks like Snow White's stepmother, I observed one day, and my grade three classmates laughed. I was clever, but Leonora was imposing: she didn't just command respect; she knew how to make herself loved. But Miss Tortosa was impervious to her seductive charm. Neither intelligence nor grace nor curiosity could sway her. Her resistance confounded us and left us powerless. The only thing she might have admired about us was something neither Leonora nor I could give her: a perfect embroidery sampler.

The embroidery sampler was a batiste rectangle on which all girls from grades one to six had to practise row after row of hemstitches, backstitches, running stitches, edging, buttonhole stitches, whipstitches – everything that ostensibly would be of use to us in our future lives as female citizens of the Argentine Republic.

There were some diligent girls who did everything well, even home economics; there were girls who were simply domestic, with magic hands for needlework; there were splendid, universally bad students who made craters instead of buttonholes almost as a matter of ideological coherence. And there were Leonora and I: to see us with needles in our hands was depressing. Miss Tortosa despised us.

I should say, since this is supposed to be a historical tale, that not everything was thankless in our home economics classes. That was where we learned the rudiments of sex with which the most intellectual of us girls would, years later, lose our virginity with revolutionary zeal, practising coitus as if demonstrating some principle: we learned that in order to have a baby, you had to blow up some white balloons (what did you blow them up with? The bearer of the news didn't know, and so, for a long time I imagined a more or less big dick emitting a sort of puff of air that could blow up a white balloon bigger and bigger until, by who-knows-what art of prestidigitation, you had a baby). We also learned that men had milk, too, only it came out of their dicks and it was poisonous, that our mothers were all whores, but mothers who had lots of kids were even bigger whores.

In general, those who brought us this information were the riff-raff, the ones who would remark, with total candour, that their aunt's brother-in-law got drunk at a party the other day and fucked his little three-year-old niece, or else they'd tell you a joke in which a hiding, naked woman provoked suggestive comments from two men passing by, to which the mother of the girl (incidentally named Pascualine) responded with the following poem:

> Smellier than a mackerel
> Smellier than a sardine
> Is the stinky pussy
> Of my daughter Pascualine.

In other words, we didn't attend Sacre Coeur; we attended a school that was so poor it didn't even have a name, located on a street which at that time, incredibly, was called Hope. And without knowing it, as we clumsily tried to perfect our whipstitch, Leonora and I were awkwardly and happily preparing ourselves for a future social and sexual revolution.

Miss Tortosa overheard our whispered conversations impassively and without curiosity. Our conduct was of no interest to her. Seated at her desk, she simply examined our efforts and showed us new stitches. That was the fatal moment for me. I remember her predatory hands, her hook-like nails, outlining the first stitches of each row on my embroidery sampler – stitches I was supposed to imitate and which she invariably made in a neat, straight line. I hated her. I knew as well as *she that as soon as I inserted the needle into the piece of batiste, chaos would invade the sampler just as it has invaded this page right now and shuffled everything I've tried to tell in such detail, the story of Leonora's tears and Miss Tortosa's stupid daughter.*

It was like this: Miss Tortosa made us stand in a line next to her desk so that she could examine our samplers. When it was Leonora's turn, she studied the piece of batiste for a long time and at last said:

"This sampler is perfect for cleaning the floor."

I went next. I don't know what awful thing she told me because it didn't catch my attention: my sampler was truly horrible, and above all, Miss Tortosa was the enemy: her rejection ennobled me. What did catch my attention was that, when I went back to my seat, I saw Leonora crying. It was a strange sight, her almond-shaped eyes wide open, and her tears falling silently down her gypsy face. Right then I realized that it was the first time I had ever seen her cry, and I realized something else: she couldn't stand not to be admired. The contempt she may have felt for Person X who didn't admire her didn't enter the picture. Or maybe I was the one who felt contempt. Because five days later, when Miss Tortosa brought her daughter to school – dressed in pink, as I recall, and with a huge bow right in the middle of her head – as soon as recess time rolled around, Leonora went over to her and, with that carefree air that made us all fall in love with her (and which I could swear was genuine), asked her if she wanted to play statues with us.

That was Leonora, able to make herself be loved by everyone: the riffraff, the "nice" girls, the school principal. From that day on, even Miss Tortosa began to love her.

"It's true," the Shark says, "you don't act like the others. The others look at us with . . . with contempt. You understand how ridiculous that is? They're atheists, they've probably screwed every Bolshevik in the city, they squeal like pigs when you poke them, and I'm sure some of them, if you gave it to them really hard, would turn in their own grandmothers, and yet they look at us with contempt. They have no sense of morality, is what I

haven't seen you around the neighbourhood for a long time. Are you married? Do you have kids?" Revealing her hunchback, her wooden leg, her puss-filled cyst, she replies that she hasn't got any kids and she's not married. "But Leonora is, right? She must have gotten married young. Are you still good friends? I saw her ages ago with a darling little girl – how old must she be now?" So this, too, is the story: young wife with a darling little girl – how old must she be now? She hasn't even seen the magazine pictures, *the five most wanted guerrilla girls; reward for any information . . . .* That face with the high cheekbones that keeps smiling at her from wherever. None of this seems to make a dent on the Villavicencio twin. Here she is, as pleased as punch, with her wretched little boy, that kid we all knew how to get. The world hasn't changed for her; keep it in mind for the next composition. Topic: the people. But she isn't the people. "And what are you doing back in the neighbourhood?" Time, she's stupidly marking time because she's assigned herself the duty (like a redemption?) of standing guard for no less than three hours in hopes of seeing the Professor, who will verify that Leonora is safe so that she can get rid of this emptiness once and for all. "We've really all gone our own ways, haven't we? Wouldn't it be great if we could have a reunion of all the girls in our class and find out what's become of everyone?" What would be even greater would be for the earth to open up and swallow the twin, for the kid to have an attack of whooping cough or for the husband to show up with a stick and beat the hell out of her, making her leave, anything to keep from having to listen to her anymore; it's remarkable that she still wants, more than anything in the world, for the twin to go away; there must be a zone of self-preservation, then, intervals or just moments when she, inside her bubble, wants more than anything for the twin to go away. "You know who I saw yesterday? I saw . . ." Please, spare me these memories of grade school, I can't take it. "She married a very successful podiatrist; she left the neighbourhood, too, but her parents still live here. What about your parents?" They're in

Tibet, they became Tibetan monks and they go around in white robes, fasting hard and in unison. "He died? Your dad died? I'm so sorry." There she is. The old woman. She's very tiny, looks like she could walk calmly through the neighbourhood, and yet . . . Hertha Bechofen! It's none other than Hertha Bechofen, the Viennese woman-who-thinks-like-a-man. She's sat down again by the window and has taken out her notebook. Please don't let her connect me with the Villavicencio twin and her wretched child. Just in case, she gives the twin a sour look. She's put on a sour face; talking to the woman with the kid seems to be annoying her. Now she's looking my way, as though she's seeking my support. If only I could find out what she's expecting to see through that window, I'd understand part of her story. The strange thing is my conviction that it would be an interesting story. Faith in myself, or in the human race? I don't think the answer matters. I'm getting old, no doubt about it, but I don't think it's so unpleasant, except for my hands. The kid is sniffling, but the woman still isn't leaving. The girl seems uneasy. She looks out the window again and seems startled. She's seen something in the house across the street: is it the man in glasses who's just left that house? She's standing up – will she make the same mistake a second time? No. Surely she wants to run out, but she's stopped to say goodbye to the young woman and the child. Now she's leaving, she's crossing the street, and walking cautiously in the same direction as the man. The young woman has taken the child's hand and is ready to leave, but she notices the notebook. She appears confused. "Leave it, I'll give it to her," I say. The man in glasses has stopped at the bus stop. The girl is standing in line, behind him, as though she hasn't noticed him. Now, right now, the man turns around and sees her. They embrace; they seem overwrought with emotion. "How are you, my child?" he says, momentarily taking her back to the days when she wished that man could be her father. What a coincidence, she says, I was just about to go visit you. He gestures with his hand, silencing her, asks her how she is, he hasn't seen her in so long. She replies that she's fine, at least as fine as one can be (lowering her voice) in times like these; what she wants is to find out if they know anything about . . . He makes the same hand gesture again. There's nothing to be done, he says. Fernando called, letting us know that Leonora didn't show up for an appointment and since then she's disappeared.

◆

Words wear out over time; they lose the sharpness of their letters. *Chair* is no longer the broken-down straw chair Diana used to climb on in order to look through the window at her grandmother's house, nor is it the uncomfortable, whimsical one in which someone (who isn't, strictly speaking, the person she is now) used to sit and write when Leonora's story – and other stories – hadn't yet devastated her face and her soul. Sometimes scraps remain, the radiance of things waiting expectantly within words, a vestige of old bakeries fleetingly scenting the word *bread*, a gust of jubilant air in the word *wind*. Or else there are fortunate words – foggy, shadow, bird, sea – that preserve intact the music of all birds or of the sea. But words nearly always become terse, more melodic or less sad or more symbolic of the precise thing that gave birth to them.

The late October afternoon when Diana ran into Professor Ordaz, the word *disappeared* had not just become limited in scope; it lacked scope entirely. It was a growing wave of lava made stronger by each contact than by any possible symbolic virtue. Until a short time before, it had possessed a clear, innocent shape, but that didn't work anymore. How could one apply the same name to a certain transitory quality of the Genie of the Magic Lantern and the present condition of the newspaper vendor whose stand had been near the University and with whom Diana used to chat about Russian literature? Now she must accommodate in neutral syllables the panicky premonition she felt when she saw the empty shelves, the nervous look of the man at the candy stand when she questioned him, the threatening silence of the guy at the ticket office, the crazy story told by the old woman who sold little whales – seen for the last time on the subway steps – a story that jumbled together trampled books, assassins with machine guns, and a peaceful, wise man who was dragged down the steps, so that her deluded monologue and the candy man's suspicious expression and the ticket vendor's silence were all interwoven with other silences and other expressions and other monologues recited *sotto voce* that would create an aura of fear around the magic word, since nothing disappears. Diana, sweetheart, people don't go up in smoke like the Genie of the Magic Lantern; then they must take them out of real life, mama, they make them vanish from our world so they can have them at their mercy – there are rumours of sticks pushed into anuses, of ravaged vaginas, of men whose tendons have been pulled so hard they can only drag themselves along like animals – they pull them from the light of day and plunge them into a bottomless nightmare because now all limits can be trespassed by those who have ceased to belong to the human race.

◆

"The newspaper guy couldn't take it," the Shark says.

"Oh, so he was a reporter?" the other one says.

"No. It's a joke. He sold newspapers at a subway stand."

Then he brings his hands to his forehead, slipping them towards his temples as though he wants to clear his head, and walks towards the prisoner's cubicle.

◆

The bus has arrived. The man wearing glasses climbs on, but the girl doesn't. She didn't even try to pretend she was at the bus stop for some reason. She remains motionless and seems lost, like someone who has misplaced an important reference. Now she's started walking; she's coming this way, but she shows no sign of entering, as if she's forgotten where she came from. She's stunned. The last picture of Leonora that she saw, her smiling face among the most wanted women, brutally superimposes itself on all her thoughts, unleashing a stream of fierce logic: if they could drag an idealistic newspaper vendor off to a nightmare from which he hasn't returned, what kind of horrors wouldn't they inflict when they have a most wanted prisoner in their hands? "Logic for a logical world," the woman who's watching her through the window of the Mecca will tell her one day. "Not applicable in times of official lunacy." She hates her body, or rather, she hates the wholeness of her body as seen from the perspective of someone who must be lying with her own body shattered. She needs to imagine that whipped flesh until she herself feels raw, to hear her howls in the darkness until she wishes to be deaf forever – *"Listen"* – since only by plunging into her own pain can she redeem herself of the strange intoxication of life.

"Listen."

She recognizes the voice and is startled. The notebook! Abject terror runs through her. Her yellow-paged notebook has fallen into the hands of the beer-bellied guy and now she will pay for her written words. Is this what I've become? she thinks, this trembling creature who worries about what she's written? And in the name of the woman who screams in the darkness, she turns around furiously.

"What is it?" she says defiantly.

She walks with determination towards the man.

"The lady." Standing at the door of the Mecca, the man points to his left, inside the café. "She asked me to get you."

Cautiously, Diana sticks half her body inside the café and looks around. The Bechofen woman is watching her fearlessly from her table by the window. With a slight movement of her index finger, she points to the notebook. Then, once Diana has entered the café, she invites her to sit down.

"You need a good cup of coffee," she says. "You look pale."

"Yes, I suppose." Diana sits. "Thanks so much."

"You don't have to thank me, dear. I'm not a good person. I mean, I'm not in the habit of picking up starving passersby on the street." She pauses. "Unless they interest me. And to be honest, your behaviour fascinates me."

"Oh, my behaviour." Diana puts herself on guard. "Nothing unusual. I was looking for someone who . . ." She cuts herself short. "I suppose I was looking for the same thing as you. Someone who interests me."

The Bechofen woman smiles. She drums her finger on the notebook, which is lying in the middle of the table.

"Ah, young writers in search of their story. Do you want some advice? Don't look for it so passionately. It might interfere with the facts and turn you into one of the characters."

"With all due respect, señora, I don't need advice."

"Don't be so sure, my dear. This is a time of great loneliness for people like you."

"I don't think that's the most serious problem of these times, loneliness, I mean."

"Don't believe it. I was young, too, in a city full of cafés. We were trying to fix the world, and we spouted philosophy in cafés. Cafés made us feel like part of something on the move. That's what I liked about Buenos Aires when I first arrived. Here, too, passion boiled over in cafés. That's why I tell myself: it must be hard to be young in a world without cafés."

"As I said, that's not the worst thing that's happening to us."

"It's not the worst thing, but it's bad. Not so much the fact that you don't feel like getting together in a café to discuss things. But that you don't feel like discussing anything, that's the bad part. It's just another very refined, very dangerous way of killing you, don't you see?"

"No, I don't see. Do you want me to tell you something? A week ago they took away my best friend, the one I talk about in here, in this notebook. And now they must be tearing her body apart, day after day, till she can't take any more. Maybe she's already given up; maybe she's already dead. Do you understand what I'm saying? There's no 'other' way of killing."

"It's worth discussing. And so is whatever's in this notebook. A guest of mine has invented a sort of imitation café. He calls it a workshop. Here's my address. Come see us."

"I don't believe in workshops."

"Neither does he. You might have fun."

◆

"Tell me about yourself."

"What do you mean?"

"You, what you were like." His eyes are fixed on his shoes, and he's jingling a ring of keys. "What you were like before you got involved in all this."

"Oh, me." She makes an effort to recall some detail worth telling; it all seems too distant. "I wore braids; I lived in a neighbourhood."

"The neighbourhood, what was it called?"

"Almagro," the prisoner says. "My parents still live there, in the same house they lived in before I was born."

"Did you have playmates?"

"Playmates? Yes, of course. Lots of playmates."

"And what games did you play? Did you play with dolls?" Unexpectedly, he lets out a little, nervous laugh as though he's said something daring or as if something was bothering him.

"Well, I didn't really like dolls too much. I preferred games . . ."

"Boys' games," she's about to say (*We liked boys' games, boys' books, the world of boys. A little brutal and a little shocking, we preferred leapfrog or cops and robbers to the serene ritual of visiting. We ardently read adventure books that were not intended for girls, and we never dreamed of being Pearl of Labuan or Sweet Ilene. We were*

72

Sandokan and Henry of Lagardere, and Prince Valiant. We aspired to being in a world of heroism, one that we were absolutely not resigned to watching from the outside. We were the heroes. Secretly, we also cried over Little Women, *but those tears didn't define us – that might have confused us with the hordes of weepers who-could-worry-who-could-care-who-could-marry-a-millionaire. We didn't want to be our mothers, and the only kind of transgression we knew was that one: the world of boys),* but she looks the Shark in the face – something about him has put her on alert – and says:

". . . that made you think. I especially liked games that made you think. The Magic Brain, and riddles. And puzzles to put together." She's remembering something that makes her light up, in spite of the chains. "I had a puzzle that I got from . . . do you know Rear Admiral Mandayo?"

The Shark seems to stand at attention.

"I've never spoken to him, but I respect him," he says.

"He's my second cousin, did you know?"

"Affirmative."

"He brought it to me from one of his trips."

"What was it like?"

"It was made of wood, but that's not really important. What matters is who gave it to me. He always liked me a lot, my cousin."

Without raising his head, the Shark observes her from under his eyebrows. When he finally speaks, it's violent.

"And why did you change?" he asks violently. "What suddenly made you turn into a . . . ? It was that rat bastard, wasn't it? That Montonero?"

The prisoner seems taken aback. "My . . . husband?" she says.

The Shark explodes: "Don't call him that. He doesn't deserve it. An assassin who made you turn against God and the Fatherland?"

73

"I never turned against God or the Fatherland. I love God. He's with me – who do you think helps me endure all this?"

The Shark nails his eyes on the prisoner with hostility. "You." He points his finger at her. "You and nobody else brought this punishment on yourself."

"And I'm paying for it. But I never turned against God. And I love the Fatherland, maybe in a different way, but just as much as you do."

"Shut up. I don't want to hear that. There's only one way to love the Fatherland. Anything else is dirtying it, like what you people wanted to do."

"I never wanted . . ."

"Shut up, I said. Tell me about before; that's what I want to know. What you were like before you became this. . . ." He runs a spiteful gaze up and down the prisoner's open body.

"I don't know. I don't understand exactly what you want to know. I was a very good student. I liked math; I was studying drawing; I read a lot."

He raises his head abruptly.

"You read?" His tone is barely threatening. "What kinds of things did you read?"

"I don't know, books about pirates, Greek mythology. I really liked Greek mythology."

For a few seconds, the only sound that can be heard is that of the Shark quickly rattling the keys.

"Why?" he says, finally. "Explain to me, if you can, why all of you read. In every house we go into – " He cuts himself short, pointing with an almost demented gesture at an invisible spot to his left. "Do you know what we find there? Books, thousands of books. You'd have to be Superman to classify them, to find out what those books did to you, why they messed up your brains like that, what you found there that made you want to destroy the Fatherland."

"We didn't want to." She corrects herself carefully: "Some of us didn't want to."

"Quiet! Don't defend them; they're criminals. The country is infested with criminals. We don't know where else to look for them anymore, in factories, in schools. A criminal might be hiding in the most unlikely corner. Do you know who the man you married is? Do you know?"

"Maybe I don't."

"He's an assassin. Did you know he was the one who blew up one of our submarines?" He stops as though waiting for a reply, but the prisoner watches him silently. "Did you know or didn't you?"

"His aides didn't usually confide in me."

The Shark raises his head, observing her slowly, as though he'd like to find out what's behind her blank face.

"But we'll find him," he says, his gaze fixed on the prisoner. "And we're going to make him pay for every one of his crimes." His lips are taut with anger. Suddenly he bursts out: "Is your daughter with him?"

"I think so."

"The poor innocent victim." Playing with the keys, he seems calmer. "Last night before I went to sleep, I thought a lot about her, about her birthday. I imagined her at a party with clowns, blowing out the ten candles . . ." He stops playing with the keys and decisively puts them away in his pocket. "What colour is her hair?"

She's blonde, like her father. The prisoner hesitates.

"Like mine," she says at last. "Maybe a little bit lighter."

"What games does she like?"

"Dolls," the prisoner says, without missing a beat.

Perhaps the skill of her own response, or something ambiguous in the Shark's expression, makes her recover a bit of confidence because this time she takes the initiative. Showing genuine interest, she asks:

75

"And you? Do you have children?"

There's an uncomfortable silence during which the prisoner regrets her question. She's trying to think of something pleasant to say when the Shark's murky voice surprises her.

"People don't always have what they want," he says.

"It's true," the prisoner says, buying time. "Now I don't have my daughter. And I would give anything to see her."

The Shark doesn't seem to hear her, as though he's gotten stuck on some previous fact. He moves a few steps forward, wrapped in his own thoughts.

"I'm sure you'd be able to understand."

Like someone who's about to tell a story, he sits down on the cot.

"Get up right now!" the prisoner shouts.

The violence of her outburst startles both of them.

You'll spill it even if I have to jab this down to your tonsils, you Montonero bitch. The man who had said it – the voice reached her through the darkness a few hours earlier – came from the same person who is now standing a few feet away from her, breathing heavily, and with such hatred in his eyes that the prisoner is terrified.

"Can't you see I'm dirty?" she shouts, and her voice is truly desperate. "It's been . . . how many days have I been here? I can't stand my own stink. Piss, sweat, shit . . . How can you bear to sit next to me?"

◆

She's gone upstairs to her apartment in an annoying state of confusion. Ever since she left the café, the body that is splayed out in some murky corner of this city stubbornly cries out inside her, or rather, she stubbornly refuses to abandon that body, like a final, desperate proof of loyalty. But, at the same time, this doesn't prevent her from feeling a bottomless rage at the indifference of Hertha Bechofen, who must still be in the Mecca drinking coffee and taking notes, phlegmatically oblivious to the fact that, in the last few months, reality has turned to nightmare. And yet it doesn't prevent her from experiencing a certain amount of curiosity, either. She's read this woman; more than once she's let herself be carried along by those apparently cold tales, in whose detailed plot the absurd passion for life burns, nonetheless; she may have seen an occasional essay of hers. ("She thinks like a man," she recalls someone having stupidly written on a back cover, and she remembers a few idiots of both sexes, deciding that the Bechofen woman thinks like neither a man nor a woman, since it can't be proved that men and women think according to gender.) She's been impressed by her pleasantly ironic comments in interviews. And now that she's seen her, she can't reconcile so many rarefied words with the small, wrinkled woman who put the atrocities of her story in doubt. *What story? Did I even tell her a story?*

In spite of herself, curiosity prevails. She takes a book from the shelf, opens it. On the flyleaf the woman looks young and no doubt about it, seductive. *That's the word* (the Bechofen woman is writing). *Seduction. I could see it in the faces of my interviewers each time I spoke. And, slyly, I depended on that seduction: I could speak "like a man" about my own view of intellectual commitment, shock them with some of my ideas, and observe how I had tenderly trapped the other person in my web. But today I tried to do the same thing and saw only indignation and surprise in the face of the girl with the notebook. She was judging me. When your face is wrinkled, you can't afford the luxury of appearing frivolous. But, what's frivolous? This? Thinking about the loss of my seductive powers, when terror has erupted here? They can't even imagine how well I know that terror. I've witnessed it to an extent they don't dare think about, even now.* She was born in Vienna in 1906, Diana reads on the flyleaf, and she came to Argentina in 1938, fleeing from the horrors of Nazism. *You've got to admit that we may not have had any other option but to think about ourselves and about the absurdity of small daily actions within the cracks History has left open to us. Although maybe it's not even that: History doesn't leave cracks open; it's always solid and complete and dominating. It's you yourself who has to widen the crack and take a peek at the small, friendly world. Ah, I once wrote that when words still flowed from me; even in frightening times, life blossoms like a wildflower, something the girl with the notebook couldn't, or wouldn't, understand. And yet there was something in her eyes, something that convinced me that at some other time, at the height of my seductiveness, I would have at least fascinated her. Maybe that's the challenge: to make her stop seeing my wrinkles.* She decides she won't go to that woman's house; she doesn't need her. In order to prove it to herself, she opens the yellow-leafed notebook. And without intending to (or perhaps because she suspects that only from that vantage point will she be able to evaluate the unhappiness of what she's about to say), she begins writing about happiness. About how by chance they had been touched by the wonderful gift of happiness.

◆

Some individuals are susceptible to purification. The mere act of kneeling before an altar or immersing themselves in prestigious waters allows them to emerge clean of all traces of the past. The Shark, in a certain sense, belongs to that species. As he leads the prisoner to the attic, where the showers are, he experiences an emotion akin to fulfillment. He has seen plenty of open flesh lately, bodies that shit themselves with fear, bleeding mouths and genitals. He's very much aware that his actions are helping to cleanse the Fatherland of a major ill. He tends to think about General San Martín, about General Roca, and feels proud that he, too, has the opportunity to serve that Argentina of the glorious past. But sometimes he feels a bit weary: his generation hasn't been given such an easy role; that's why the prisoner's words have shaken him. Can't you see

I'm dirty? He must wash away this woman's filth as well as her mistakes: he feels – he's had a chance to notice – that there's good stuff in her which will allow her to progress. His determination is much more than an act of obedience. "She's one of the worthwhile ones and can be rehabilitated," the Falcon told him. "I'm putting you in charge of her." His determination is an act of purity.

In a different sense, this is an act of purification for the prisoner, as well. Even though I took many other baths after that one, she will explain to me one day, I've never had such a perfect feeling of cleanliness as I did that afternoon. After a week in the basement, I could see the light of day for the first time, but most of all, I felt water for the first time. The water ran over my naked body, washing away the sweat and urine and days of shitting in a bedpan, and days of shitting on myself, and the mark of the chains, and the pain and fear. All the filth in the universe was washed away by the water. I raised my head and let it run down my face and my hair, and it was a blessing. *As if it were purifying us* (Diana writes, determined to set in words what they had been like, what sort of scheme of happiness defined them, now that one of the two is about to be lost or perhaps has already been lost forever), *as if its happy tune were resounding just for us. We would run through the streets, splashing in puddles; we let our clothing and our school smocks get soaked; we would laugh like maniacs at those prudent people who carried umbrellas; we howled and sang and laughed in the rain. And we raised our faces to the sky to receive full face the celestial gift of water.*

Later, her body clean and dry and wrapped in a big, white terrycloth robe with the Marine emblem on it, she is led by the Shark to a place to the right of the bathrooms. They enter a very spacious room that he refers to as the whisky locker.

"Pick out whatever you want," he says, pointing all around him at enormous piles of diverse objects whose nature cannot yet be discerned in detail.

"What's a whisky locker?" asks the prisoner, who has always been curious and who, for the first time in a long time, feels relaxed.

"It's a nautical term," the Shark says. "The whisky locker is the compartment of a ship where weapons, food, and other things are stored."

In the pile she goes through with the Shark's assistance, they find no food, and no weapons, either. In whimsical disarray and in the order in which they remove them, they find several pairs of jeans, three or four blouses, a little girl's dress, a T-shirt with the word *Peace* surrounded by flowers, another with Che's picture, some grease-stained overalls, a teacher's smock, slippers of various sizes, an old woman's shoe, some skates, a ridiculous, flouncy *quinceañera* dress.

The prisoner chooses simple, comfortable clothing. She's never been one for ostentation.

Seven

The basement compartments are separated by partitions and are mostly used for interrogations, so that a person in one of them (lying, let's say, on a metal cot or a folding bed) will be able to hear simultaneously all the sound effects produced in the others, assuming they can heard over the level of the music (not necessarily music: it might be a football game, a cartoon, or some other distraction). This capacity to be heard over the music is frequently observed in the voices of those who are interrogated, although it might be incorrect to call them "voices": in almost all cases, they're inarticulate sounds, difficult to qualify with a name. Howls? Bellows? They burst forth suddenly or else drag out over time until the listener gets the impression that the throat emitting them is about to close like a fist. Occasionally, however, the interrogated subject will articulate sounds on exhalation, returning him to his human condition in the ear of the listener. These emissions may be simply a scream – crying out to one's mother or to God – a blasphemy, or a plea. They may also take the form of a confession: names or places that seem to have been yanked out of the emitter's guts and which, in certain cases, the habituated listener lying on the cot might consider inconsistent, as if the interrogated subject, having crossed the threshold of the tolerable, or *in extremis* (imminent death, insanity) – just as a drowning

81

man grabs one who's still afloat – had seized upon that neighbour lady who attended demonstrations, or a cousin who quoted Lenin, or an office mate who grew pale every time he heard a siren. On those occasions when the emitted information does not seem inconsistent, the recumbent listener may be able to detect subsequent activity, hear orders, and even anticipate the imminent departure of a car or two. In those cases where the information (this can also occur) is proffered good-naturedly and with little previous interrogation, the recumbent listener might hear only the subsequent activity and the orders, since the discourse itself, generally extensive, is expressed in a nearly normal tone of voice, or rather, it lacks those qualities described earlier that would render it audible over the music. In this sense it resembles the discourse of the interrogators. Not in length, no: the interrogator's emissions are brief and precise, as the recumbent listener will detect during a pause in the music – *We've got your daughter. Is this the first time someone's ripped your asshole open? Zap her in the cunt again – this one's about to give it up* – except when, due to unprofessional circumstances (a fit of fury, a personal thirst for revenge), the interrogator's voice rises above a normal level.

Interrogations aren't the only activities that take place in the basement, but the woman lying on a cot, chained, has no way of knowing this. She can only distinguish what can be heard in the distance – music on the radio, cries, fragments of interrogations – or, at times, whatever happens to cross her field of vision, since her blindfolded condition – if the recumbent woman is lucky – might not be permanent. In the strictest sense, almost nothing is permanent in this section since, according to what the recumbent woman can distinguish, subjects are taken away once the session is over or in the event of death. The electrical equipment can be observed on a small table near the cot. Anyone lying there, chained, would be perfectly able to deduce, if observant enough, that all the compartments must have similar equipment and that other instruments – clubs, pliers, scalpels for pulling off skin – must be brought in especially for certain sessions. The lighting – logically, since it's a basement – is always artificial.

The attic, on the other hand, has natural lighting in almost all sections, and the functions carried out there vary. Exiting the bathroom, on the right, we find the large area they call the *whisky locker*, where material obtained from searches is stored. Not everything: the room wouldn't hold all of it. Televisions, small appliances, and furniture of any value can be utilized by officials and their families or sold by personnel recruited for this purpose. As for the books, they are too numerous and are assumed to be of interest, so they are stored in a special wing of the basement for subsequent classification and analysis, although it seems unlikely that any of the many books brought in would yield any useful conclusion: Titans of Universal Poetry, Heart, Robinson Crusoe, Chronicle of Poor Lovers, La Nausée, *we are made of all these. How can anyone speak of us without speaking of the books? One could trace an itinerary of our souls by naming them, one by one, resurrecting the fury with which we – daggers between our teeth – hurled ourselves overboard in order to recover the Pearl of Labuán, the gleeful daring with which we rescued Anna of Austria's diamonds, the sense of justice with which, in Sherwood Forest, faithfully flanked by Little John and the rest of our retinue, we robbed the treasure of Landless John's courtiers to feed the poor. We were sisters of the outcast Huckleberry Finn, we abhorred the police in the name of Jean Valjean, trembling, we asked: Stone upon stone, and where was man? And we intoned, like a lovely, hopeful melody, that a spectre is haunting Europe. We, or some of us (those who never stooped over in the sugarcane plantations of Tucumán or broke our backs in the* mate *plantations of Misiones, or raised fifteen starving kids, or lacked leisure and a beautiful library in which to enjoy it, but who one day learned how to make the cause of those men and women our own), we began to learn, among the adventures, of heroism and loyalty and ethics and justice in those books. They – those books themselves – were our adventure and our sustenance.* There are also encyclopedias, art history books, children's stories, scientific texts, a great pagestorm. The assistance of those prisoners who are qualified and willing to serve in their classification is very useful.

The prisoners occupy the left wing. Most of them are concentrated in two large areas untouched by natural light (in any event, such light would be of little use to them since they're blindfolded all the time). There are so many of them that, although they themselves are unaware of it, they produce a generalized thrum – a sort of faint moan – and a generalized odour that causes revulsion as soon as one enters. In some cases, if one listens carefully and as long as no guard is around, bits of truncated dialogue can be detected beneath the moan. Snippets of phrases in which someone tries to explain to someone else who he was, or enquires about loved ones, or asks the new arrival about things on the outside, as if an eternity separated him from the world of the living. Fragments beneath the general din that establish a complex network of information which, except for a few threads that manage to filter outside, will end up buried right there among the quiet bodies and the nauseating smell.

The residents of these sectors remain permanently chained in place, except during those intervals when they're taken to the basement for interrogation. Some of them don't come back, but this isn't sufficient to make room for the new contingents that are brought in every day. Sporadically, some chained prisoner or other is moved to another section of the establishment or is dumped in a deserted area and left for the police to discover. The others are summoned according to a list, once a week, usually on Wednesdays. Of course, no one tells them that they're going to be killed.

The rest of the left wing is comprised of small cells occupied by higher-ranking prisoners who demonstrate a certain co-operative spirit. Here, the light is natural. There's no visible landscape because the windows are very high up, but there *is* sky, a small rectangle of sky in which, on clear nights, one can spy a star. And that's enough for one to be happy, as long as one possesses, of course, a healthy dose of inner joy.

"Were those her exact words? Did she really say 'inner joy'?"

"That's what she meant. And she spoke of birds. Of what if means to hear a bird sing when one has been in a basement for many days. And of some very lovely photos she had stuck on the walls. And of the incomparable happiness of having her hands free."

But not her legs. Her legs are fastened by cuffs that are chained to a cannonball. If she lifts the cannonball, she can move, with difficulty. She no longer requires a bedpan: when necessary, a guard leads her to the bathrooms and, once a week, they take her for a shower. Another advantage of this new situation is that she can't hear the howling anymore. Occasionally someone they've come for will go crazy. *Enough! Not again! I can't take it anymore!* Or else in the middle of the night, she might hear a voice firmly reading off a list of numbers, and immediately thereafter the sound of many chains dragging. At those times it's hard for her to fall asleep. She stares fixedly at the Polynesian woman with flower garlands against an intensely blue sky, until at last she calms down and goes to sleep. But what calms her most is the work. The work was offered to her by the Falcon, and in a strict sense, it's what has brought her up from the basement to the attic.

◆

The work doesn't seem to calm her. She leafs through the yellow-paged notebook and slams it shut. For the last week, she's done nothing but waver between the reconstitution of a distant – and chemically pure – joy, in which she doesn't always believe, and an ambiguous horror that dissolves as soon as she names it. One which perhaps is nothing but my own horror, she thinks, horrified, since the other horror, the one experienced by a woman whom she sometimes imagines as dying and other times as dead, is something she knows precious little about. And her joy? *Could I be evoking my own joy? And isn't it my own tree, mine alone, that's fallen on my own head?*

I'm fed up with myself, she thinks absent-mindedly. And perhaps in order to inflict punishment on her own self-sufficiency, or because she doesn't know what to do with so many napkins or yellow sheets of paper haphazardly bearing fragments of nothing, or simply because she wants to scream out loud for help, violating her pride, she searches in her purse for the scrap of paper on which the Bechofen woman had written her address.

◆

As for personal activities, if we understand as such those that complete and justify us, torture only partially satisfies the Falcon. It's true he considers it necessary, even essential – in that sense he's convinced that technical perfection and personal adaptation yield quicker and more thorough results than the mere mechanical application of certain rote procedures, which is why he pays special attention to evaluating his subordinates – yet it isn't the task itself that gives him pleasure, but rather the verification of certain predictions. He considers himself to be a psychologically astute man; up to this point he can boast of having judged correctly in a high percentage of cases. He requires only one reply in an interview, a slight trembling of hands, some arch expression, to figure out who will sing right away, who will be willing to co-operate, who will hold out until he bursts like a toad, inflated with heroism or unmitigated hatred, before he'll say a single word. For this exclusive purpose he finds it useful to attend or even conduct torture sessions every once in a while – direct contact with the facts tends to give him a good basis for evaluation – but the spectacle doesn't gratify his senses as much as his intelligence. He enjoys proving that, according to his assumptions, stimulus X applied to subject Y always yields effect Z.

In this regard he differs from those colleagues who experience genuine, direct pleasure during the act. The Falcon secretly feels contempt for those individuals even though he recognizes that the ones who dig their hands into the dough are the most creative, a fact that turns out to be quite useful: carried along by their desire for personal satisfaction, they can be capable of improvising most effectively. And this doesn't even take into account the fact that the interrogated subjects usually note their torturers' delight in crossing a threshold of pain or carrying out a previously unimaginable torment, which intensifies the destructive effect. Nonetheless, the Falcon relies more on men like the Shark. The Shark doesn't feel any pleasure when he's torturing: he feels pride. He has a mission to fulfill and he fulfills it. Each time he makes a prisoner talk, he takes one step forward in his commitment to cleanse Argentina of unpatriotic Marxist dogs with internationalist tendencies. A commitment that requires our sacrifice (he said one day when whisky had made him more talkative than usual), and which is no more and no less noble, no more and no less necessary, than crossing the Andes or the sinking of Spanish galleons by Admiral Brown. Other times, other methods, but the same spirit of serving the Fatherland. Men like the Shark are more useful because they follow all orders to the letter.

In any event, pleasure or pride is a simple nuance, a mere subjective manifestation. And torture is simply one of many methods for fulfilling a plan that is nobler and more ambitious than the extermination of a few men. That's not enough for the Admiral; he wants something more transcendent, something higher: he wants Power. That's why, even though men like Sixfingers can't understand it, his directives go beyond coarseness, beyond the only thing that attracts the mediocre: the elimination of traitors. His directives aim above all at the utilization of redeemable material. And in this sense, the Falcon might be considered to be the Admiral's right-hand man, above a rear admiral like Sixfingers, despite Sixfingers's higher rank at the Naval Academy. Out of all possible roles, the Falcon's has been the loftiest, that of Chief of Intelligence. He knows, better than anyone else, that beneath this roof lie ability and knowledge. And he also knows how to root them out. And how to manipulate them. He's made no mistake about the Montonera: from the first interrogation he's suspected what he might expect from her. Even beyond her cousin Rear Admiral Mandayo's personal interest in the case, beyond the Admiral's negotiations with her father's associates, he's recognized in her a version of himself. He's followed her progress closely, and, through the Shark's reports, he's realized that the opportunity to entrust her with the task has arrived. He's already convinced that he hasn't misjudged her.

◆

It wasn't a good beginning. The Bechofen woman lives in a fourth-floor walk-up ("In Paris you'd find it charming," she told her as they climbed the stairs, but they're not in Paris), and as soon as they walked in, she ushered her into the kitchen where the Bechofen woman resumed an apparently interrupted activity: peeling celery, leeks, carrots, and other vegetables. And to make matters worse, sitting on a little stool that's too short for his legs, a long-nosed guy who reminds her of Kierkegaard and who won't leave them alone even for a moment, has just said something about the literary workshop that he apparently leads, an irritating fact since Diana has no confidence in literary workshops – in fact, she regards them with disdain. That's what I liked about you right away, Kierkegaard (real name: Garita) will tell her a month later; I find them despicable, too. A few years ago I would have made mincemeat of anyone who mentioned them. But that's life: sometimes it leads you to accept things you would have found unacceptable before – and he will wiggle his snaky fingers. The question is, up to what point, right? To which Diana, neither abruptly nor expansively, will reply: What? And do you think there's a limit to what's acceptable? And perhaps that's the real subject of the story. Of *my* story, of course. Because the story Diana attempts to synthesize for the Bechofen woman that afternoon in 1976 (ignoring Garita), as the woman-who-thinks-like-a-man stands over the sink, energetically peeling various vegetables, is one of evocation, heroism, and tragedy.

It's about, she says, someone who has been close to her for years — intimately close, she says, and the Bechofen woman momentarily raises her eyebrows — and who has died. (And she realizes that perhaps she's simplifying the facts a little, or hiding the problem that's brought her to this kitchen: not knowing the ending, advancing and retreating in a shadowy zone, thrashing about in death throes that never kill outright. But how could the old vegetable-scraper and the long-nosed man with butterfly hands help her if she begrudges them the only question she would like to express: how to tell a story when you don't know the ending?)

"How did she die?" Garita asks. He's smoking a cigarette that seems to crumble between his fingers, and every so often, he takes a slug of whisky from a glass he then rests on the floor.

"It doesn't matter how she died," Diana says so decisively that she nearly believes it herself. "What matters is our friendship, the time of that friendship. A very special time; I mean, we actually saw the milkman's last wagon and we touched the revolution with our hands. And one fine day we realized we had lost everything: the wagon and the revolution. Leonora represents that time."

"How did she die?" Garita repeats, unfazed. He takes a slow drag of the cigarette. Diana's nostrils flare to attention. Marijuana.

"It doesn't matter how she died," she says furiously. "What matters is what died along with her." And she understands that even greater than her anger at Longnose is her fury at the old woman who has brought her to this kitchen and hasn't said boo.

89

"A time that was too splendid, too filled with emotion, to let it slip through your fingers," and she looks despairingly at her open hands as if something were really escaping and couldn't be stopped.

Then there's a slight change that puts Diana on alert from head to toe. The old vegetable-scraper speaks for the first time. Diana doesn't breathe: she wants to drink in those words that might hold the solution to what is happening. But it's impossible. She's just discovered to her horror that what the woman said was in German. And now she's silent. Unhurriedly, as though nothing has happened, she continues peeling.

"What did she say?" Diana asks Garita, with more anxiety than she'd like to reveal.

He looks at her with a dreamy expression. Then he looks at the tiny woman who's working over the sink.

"She said she really likes leeks," he replies.

And he takes a slug of whisky and another slow, sensual drag on the cigarette.

Eight

It had to do with a special mission. A certain device – unique in the entire country and absolutely essential to the National Meteorological Service – needed to be calibrated in Washington, and only someone very capable and trustworthy could transport it. The National Commission of Geophysical Research chose the most brilliant and determined of its young researchers. On May 15, 1971, the chosen one left for the airport. In a padded attaché case she carried the device, and in her personal suitcase were three hundred pounds sterling in gold which had been seized by the Tupamaros in a bank robbery a few days before. Forget about exchanging them around here, they had told her; in Uruguay and Argentina gold coins are just an eccentricity, flashy jewellery for ladies. And they had handed them over to her in a discreet little cosmetics bag.

At the airport she had an unpleasant surprise. Three days earlier, a flight to Cuba had been hijacked: there was an order to inspect all passengers' luggage.

She stood in the long line of travellers who waited with their baggage. She observed that the inspection was very thorough, and she studied the inspector carefully. He looked like the baker who used to live across the street from her old house: an ill-tempered man, but whenever she smiled at him – braids hanging down her back, her white bread-bag in hand – he would give her a caramelized sugar doughnut. Men aren't too different from one another, she thought, they simply have different functions.

The inspector had close-knitted brows; he didn't even look at her when she greeted him pleasantly, depositing the two bags on the platform. Nonetheless, she flashed a broad, shopper's smile, momentarily directed at nothing in particular. She held that smile while the man opened the attaché case and attentively read the Commission's certificate that she had just handed him, and meanwhile he opened the suitcase, rummaging through her clothing with displeasure. When the man touched the cosmetics case, his expression seemed to light up with a spark of interest. He lifted the bag, hefted it in his hands, and knitted his brow even more.

"What do you have in this bag?" he asked harshly. And he raised his head.

The broad smile awaited him.

"Coins," she said in a voice that was jovial through premeditation and practice. "Argentine coins to give to some friends up north as souvenirs."

The man fingered the bag again, undoubtedly trying to verify its contents. "Elementary, my dear Watson," she would report on her return. "The man was looking for weapons, not coins. And as it turned out, what he was touching through the plastic was none other than coins. Piles of coins. Exactly three hundred, to give to some friends up north as souvenirs. He wasn't about to make a fool of himself by opening the bag, you see, so he congratulated me on my cleverness in finding such a lovely, inexpensive gift, and he wished me luck."

But the best thing, she would tell them, happened in Washington, at the third exchange bureau. "Because you have to understand that at the first one I only dared exchange twenty pounds sterling, and at the second, thirty; but when I saw they didn't find anything unusual about it, I got braver at the third one."

"I'd like to exchange some sovereigns."

"How many?"

"Two hundred and fifty."

There was a great commotion, she said. Apparently they were short of gold (she later deduced) because the employee said, *just a moment, please,* and disappeared through a door, quite upset. And she felt like she was standing on hot coals, but the employee returned, opened a carved door, and bowing slightly, escorted her into a room with red velvet carpeting and gilded mouldings on the walls. And a man in a tuxedo invited her to sit in an armchair that was like a throne and went out of his way to be attentive. And she had behaved like a lady. If only you knew, oh, if only you knew, she thought. And she laughed to herself.

She's not laughing now. She isn't revealing certain details of the incident, either; she's cast them aside as superfluous. The Admiral was very specific in his demands, and the Falcon has relayed these to her: an exhaustive report on the Organization, from its beginnings. He's particularly interested in their methods of recruiting followers, their *modus operandi*, and above all, their ideological discourse, what they wanted, how they expressed it, why people believed them. That's the point (and the Falcon drummed on the table three times with his index finger): why people believed them; you're intelligent and you must understand. Prepare an analysis. The Admiral probably isn't interested (although the Falcon didn't say so) in the methods used to seduce an airport inspector nor in her discreet little laugh amid the red velvet and gold, nor in the party atmosphere: Fernando was there that afternoon, and the Thrush was there, too, and also the skinny guy who got killed in Trelew later on, and the handsome, fearless commander who was her secret lover and who's no longer around, and others that . . . who knows? . . . when she, on her return, related the scene and they all celebrated with great

whoops of laughter because the revolution was a possible dream –
as those who were there that afternoon believed – and also an
adventure that those few, out of all mankind, were boldly taking
on. For that reason, or because her memory is shaky, or because
she's pressured by time, she has omitted the inspectors and the
gilded décor from her account; on the other hand, she has
emphasized: 1) the customary collaboration among organizations; 2) the different ways of making contact; 3) specific situa-
tions (with examples) in which personal prestige could and did
serve the militants; 4) resources for bringing material in or out of
the country. Points that would interest the Admiral. "On May
30, I was back in the country with dollars for the Tupamaros. A
month and a half later, my husband and I went into hiding," she
concludes. And before continuing with the next chapter, "In
Hiding," in order to take a breather or to reward herself for writing uninterruptedly for six hours, she stares fixedly and with pleasure at the Polynesian woman with garlands of flowers on her
chest, who, standing between a dove and three Dutch girls, stares
placidly back at her from an immensely blue sky.

•

It wasn't a good beginning, and what followed was worse. Garita
wasn't drinking normally. He was drinking – she would explain
on a different night – like only those of the Sixties generation
used to drink, people who were convinced they had to do everything to the extreme: writing, or fucking, or making a revolution,
or hanging themselves. As for the Bechofen woman, as soon as
she had scraped and peeled everything that was scrapeable or
peelable, she cut it all up into tiny pieces and threw it into a large
pot. Inopportunely, Diana thought of Hansel and Gretel; without
even trying, she imagined the old woman sticking her and Garita
into the pot. At least she couldn't think of any other reason for
having dragged her to this house and for keeping this drone cling-
ing to her skirts.

She partially understood the reason for the drone when the vegetable soup began to emit its pleasant fragrance of leeks. Earlier, they had spoken of cafés, of the need (according to Bechofen) for girls like you to get together with your peers in these frightening times. Like in the catacombs, she added with a little laugh, stirring the soup with an enormous wooden spoon, so that Diana, despite the fact that the simile tempted her and she wanted to let herself be carried along by such a lovely idea and think that, from now on, she'd have a refuge in which to alleviate her uncertainty, couldn't decide if the Bechofen woman was being serious or if she was mocking her a little, and so, when the soup began to disperse its inviting aroma and the Bechofen woman formally invited her to attend Garita's work-shops, she felt only half-relieved, a kind of relief that would dis-sipate and disappear in a few minutes when Garita, after filling his glass with whisky again (he must have been on his tenth) said *ritual day*, and nothing could stop him, until the soup arrived.

◆

The three dancing girls – colourful costumes, little Dutch caps, a jar brimming with milk – come from the magazine that carried the complete account of the Garín assault, and the Picasso dove was from a children's publication that undoubtedly got there by mistake. It doesn't contribute a great deal to the purpose of the report: a fervent editorial, a poem dedicated to Che (for obvious reasons, she can't even decorate her wall with it); a report about a Guatemalan musician who wrote the opera *We Will Go Back to the Mountain;* a few stories; and a miscellaneous section called *Cronopios.* The dove occupied the centrefold; the prisoner hadn't even asked the Shark's permission to stick it on the wall. With the three little milkmaids she had asked, and also with the Polynesian woman who had been cut out of the magazine that reported the fires at the Minimax supermarket chain, and with the blond little boy who was kissing the black child, a photo that illustrated a report on her *compañero*, the founder of the Revolutionary Armed Forces, dead in combat, a report that bore an ironic caption that she cut away. But in all instances, the Shark had given her the same reply: she could cut out whatever she liked as long as there was no information on the back that might be of interest to Intelligence. The proviso is fairly vague, the prisoner concludes. Up till now they've only taken her down once to the basement where printed material is kept: she had a bird's eye view of everything from *Anna Karenina* to *Tom Thumb*. Which texts, which fragments of those texts, might be considered to be of interest to Intelligence? (*Romain Rolland's* The Enchanted Soul? Treasure Island? The Age of Reason? *In which of those books did we learn to be rebels? Which ones whispered in our ears, in our ears only, that there are men who oppress other men, and that it isn't right? What was it? The nocturnal activities of Léon de France, the freedom that rolls through* The Pirate's Song? *What written page led us to capture the music – because at first it was music, everything is music at first, the vague perception of something noble and beautiful lying nascent within words – the violent music that stirs in the phrase, "A spectre is haunting Europe?" How did we prepare ourselves? Drinking in Almafuerte's fierce diatribes or Bécquer's unforgettable poems? Ah, Bécquer's poems – can anyone understand the joy of being sixteen years old and singing from the very centre of one's heart: "Today heaven and earth smile on me / today the sun reaches the depth of my soul / today I saw her, I saw her and she looked at me / Today I believe in God"? Breathing in those words, becoming intoxicated with them, one so loves humanity that one is willing to give up one's life for humanity's happiness.*

And now I remember "Anita, the Little Match Girl." She was in a book with a yellow cover and blue letters that said, Tales of Hans Christian Andersen. *It told the story of a little beggar girl who sold candlewicks (because in my memory there are no matches, only candlewicks, and that, too, the word "candlewicks," is a little light twinkling in my memory); a child who ends up dying of hunger and cold next to a lighted window. It's Christmas Eve, and behind that window, a happy family is celebrating. Everything worthy of being desired by people is behind that window. But Anita is on the other side of the glass, and she hasn't managed to sell a single box of candlewicks all day so that she might buy a simple piece of bread. She's hungry, she's cold, and she has a completely unreasonable desire to be happy. Then she makes herself a little party. One by one, she lights all her candlewicks. And so, illuminated by a succession of flickering lights, she celebrates her Christmas until she dies.*

What zone of emotion was forever lighted in me? How did I recognize, behind the facts, all the fear and sadness lurking in a word that didn't yet matter to me, the word "injustice"? At times I think it was precisely that day, with my eyes teary at Anita's lonely death, my heart laden with bitterness at those who, on the other side of the window, didn't even notice her death, that day when something began to build up inside me that years later I would call, as if it were the most natural thing in the world, my "ideology."

("Come on, come on, isn't that a bit of an exaggeration?" Garita will soon say. "Isn't it at the very least an extreme projection of your own obsession to attribute that metamorphosis – Anita the Match Girl transfigured with revolutionary zeal – to all the little readers who later will become Your Generation, or rather, in a certain sense, mine? And, my dear, that's not even counting all the tots in the peaceable Fifties who never read the heroic adventures of Little Red Riding Hood and who were as hungry as your Match Girl, so if they learned about social resentment anywhere, it wasn't in *The Watchmaker Monkey*."

"I'm not that naïve!" Diana will shout, so furiously that the Bechofen woman, with a calming look to make her lower her voice, will peek out from the kitchen, where she's preparing something that smells like ginger. "But even for those of us who didn't go hungry, those books had something to say. And I'm telling the story of Leonora, not the story of Humanity.")

The prisoner has read many of these books and knows that it isn't easy to categorize them according to any criterion that might be useful to Intelligence, so she put the dove on the wall without noticing what was on the back of it. And without asking the Shark's permission. If the Shark knew that it was by Picasso – the artist's signature was there, and he liked to look at the pictures on the walls whenever he came by – and that Picasso was a Communist, the fact mustn't have seemed very important to him because he didn't comment. In the case of the white child kissing the black child, he did: "This is typically subversive," he said when she showed him the picture. But the prisoner sweetly explained that it was about children, and children, thanks to their innocence, are all brothers. She had already noted that the subject of childhood was crucial. And just yesterday, noticing that after only twenty days her work was progressing at an unprecedented rate and that the walls were filling up with such pretty pictures, the Shark had to admit that the prisoner's initiative impressed him as being very positive: decorating her cell shows a high probability of rehabilitation, a fact respected as much by him as by his superiors.

◆

Friday, ritual day, Garita said. A day when my dear artist friends used to gather in a café on Corrientes, friends who were willing to go to their deaths for an adjective and who were capable of banging heads over Sartre's declaration in Paris that, compared to a child dying of hunger, *La Nausée* is insignificant.

That's what they were like, he said, or that's what he now believed they were like; then he took another swig, looked at Diana as though he were looking at a far-away object, seemingly about to pronounce one of his corrosive phrases, but instead just humming, parodying Yves Montand, *Que reste-t-il de nos amours / Que reste-t-il de ces beaux jours*. These days they talk differently, think differently, even get drunk differently; you'll meet them, he said. They're the kind who arrived at the party – or what they dreamed of as the party – too late, because I don't want to disappoint you, but I'm telling you that as for me personally, all that revolutionary fervour turned out to be too cloying. The problem is that guys like me are always born in the wrong century (he laughed); no matter when our turn comes, we're doomed to live with our contemporaries. And do you know what the problem is with our contemporaries? It's their need to find meaning in the times they happen to live in – and therefore in themselves. Which prevents them from noticing that what they call reality is just a miserable, shapeless blob, impervious to any kind of thought, and distorted, besides, by the dominant ideas of each period that hover like fog and penetrate everything. So don't take me too seriously if one day, instead of tranquillity, I'm overcome by the wine of solidarity or the muscat of nostalgia and I tell all my comrades I made them come over on Fridays in homage to the good old days. The truth is that in the good old days, I was the same as I am now: the olive in the whipped cream."

"A real son-of-a-bitch," Diana murmured, looking out of the corner of her eye at the Bechofen woman, who had just lifted the lid of the pot and was staring into it with an intense expression. "That's what I think you are."

"That's what they said, too. And worse things. Or things that sounded worse in that golden age. Because, strange as it may seem, owning the meaning of your own existence is also empowering, faith is empowering, so a guy like me became a pariah of the revolutionary age. Or an aristocrat, depending on how you look at it. It's too bad that with this band of murderers in the government, even aristocrats like me had no choice other than to accept a little solidarity. They take away your pathos, among other things. I mean, practically any afternoon, walking down the street I run into one of those café zealots who used to talk about the subversive novel and wanted to eat me alive – or the ones I wanted to eat alive, let's be honest – and we embrace as if we were the only survivors of a shipwreck. And in a sense, we are. Those of us who stayed here out of lethargy. Because there's a kind of lethargy that consists of not going – not going to work, not going to a party, not going to Europe – those of us who stayed here simply out of lethargy and are still alive. So don't get too worked up when Hertha talks about catacombs. Sometimes that Viennese woman has faith in mankind, and besides, her simile isn't even original. But, the truth of the matter is, I didn't set all this up so that the survivors could come and talk to me about what's forbidden on the outside. I set it up because the institute where I taught doesn't exist anymore, and I left the University on my own because it made me sick. I had to live somehow, didn't I? So I allowed the Austrian to take me under her wing, and here you have me, practically a relic, preaching in the catacombs."

Just then the Bechofen woman, who had silently set the table, filled three large bowls with her fragrant vegetable soup, and they sat down to eat.

◆

There's also a Christmas tree, kittens in a basket, a drawing by William Blake, a photo of some Coya Indians from the Bolivian borderlands, a picture of Marilyn Monroe blowing out candles, Dalí's Christ, the little Quaker Oats man, and all sorts of landscapes: forests, snowy fields, seascapes and moonscapes, suggesting worlds dizzyingly open beyond the little room where, for twenty-one days the prisoner has been passionately and purposefully working for the Admiral, editing a story that was her story. Except for certain omissions: her hatred of all oppressors when she read Jacques Romain's The Governors of the Dew; the pounding of her heart when she turned in the card that made her a member of the Youth Federation of the Communist Party; her little leap of joy when she discovered that socialism was beginning to take root not far away, on an island, long and green as a lizard, and that it was a hurricane that would spread through Peru and Bolivia and Nicaragua and through Argentina, too; the suspenseful vigil as they waited – with their hearts in their throats – for the first major Revolutionary Armed Forces attack to be carried out; their strange delight later, as they learned that fifteen flashy Yankee supermarkets, the perfect symbol (the prisoner had written) of imperialist penetration in our country, had exploded one after another at five-minute intervals in an impeccable, perfect operation, without a single victim. And another bit of joy, one she perhaps doesn't recognize or may consider superfluous, *the joy we all felt, those of us who had been surprised by something unprecedented in these lands, something we thought would be a good way to undermine General Onganía's dictatorship, as we wondered, a little bit hopeful and a little bit bewildered, where it all would lead.* Strictly speaking, while she enthusiastically writes, she begins to forget all happiness except this, working from morning till night in her cell – bare-walled, at first – with its high, little window through which one can see a rectangle of sky, and at times, listening hard, hear a bird singing. With nothing to tie her down but a cannonball chained to her left leg.

Her memory doesn't wander: pragmatically, she has dictated neither more nor less than what the Admiral desires from this report: tactics for expanding the initial group, planning and execution of activities, military training, connections and cooperative actions with other organizations, how and why a leftist group would join one that was obviously Peronist, theoretical foundations.

It's strange: this last part was the hardest one for her to reconstruct. She was able to reproduce exactly the diagram she made years ago for seizing an arsenal; she's made note of the words – and even the tone and suggestive jokes – with which she instructed the novices in the urban guerrilla's essential tasks: robbing a van, placing a bomb, loading a rifle, carrying a cyanide capsule in a ring or in the crown of a tooth or in a shirt button to use in case of capture, since no one knows his own limits and death is preferable to betrayal. But she has trouble recalling why these acts have meaning for her, the reason why she felt clean and generous while carrying them out, the dream for which so many people her age, or even much younger, had abandoned their daily rituals. For this reason, not for the pictures, she had asked for the magazines ten days ago. They had to be down there, she said, among the thousands of books that piled up day after day: *Militancy*, and *Christianity and Revolution*, and so many others that they – the one who died in combat, and the one they killed in Trelew, and the one who's in Europe, and the Thrush, and she herself – had used to explain to revolutionary-fevered men and women why, in their name and against the violence of power and towards the destruction of a military apparatus that oppresses people and violates the constitution of a popular government, no other method remains than to take up arms. The business of the pictures began almost accidentally. In an excess of zeal, or perhaps by mistake, they began to bring popular magazines upstairs to her as well, particularly general-interest weeklies with colourful reports on sweeps and kidnappings. She found the Polynesian woman in a Minimax Market flyer: there were garlands of flowers draped over her naked breasts and in the background a sky so blue that for a few minutes, Leonora stared at it, mesmerized. She thought it would be lovely to have it before her eyes always. The Shark himself brought her the Scotch tape and a pair of children's scissors.

A fascinating job and something beautiful to look at: what more could someone who had almost lost her life desire? She found the other pictures later. And now here they are: the three Dutch girls, Dalí's Christ, Blake's hanged man, and the little Quaker Oats man, protecting her, as the prisoner specifies the secret hiding places they had set up, how they raised their children, the resources they used to communicate with "legal" citizens, so focused on her task that she doesn't even notice the

Shark, who, as on other occasions, has stealthily entered and is staring at the pictures on the walls.

The sound of ripping paper startles her.

"What's all this garbage?"

She stands up so quickly that she trips.

"What's all what? Please, I was working." She looks like someone who has been slapped awake from a pleasant dream.

"This. This garbage." The Shark practically shakes the torn paper in her face. "Who wrote this garbage?"

The prisoner sees the empty space on the wall: *A Letter to My Son.* She had liked it because it talked about some doves outside their cage and a world without bars that a child was going to know. Written in prison in 1972, it said at the bottom, only the prisoner had cut that line out, thinking that was sufficient.

"I don't know who wrote it," she says. "I put it up because it was pretty. It talked about little doves."

"Little doves," the Shark repeats with contained fury. "You turned out to be a liar, after all, just like all the others." He wields the wadded paper like someone brandishing the *corpus delicti.*

"I don't know why you say that," the prisoner says. "It seems to me I've given sufficient proof . . ."

"You can *never* give sufficient proof. Get that through your head." He looks at the paper with revulsion. "Do you know what it says here? It says things it's not supposed to say. Especially not in a poem."

"It's about a father who dreams of a world . . ."

"*Shut up!* It talks about torture. Spells it right out: t-o-r-t-u-r-e. It's forbidden to write about that, understand? It's immoral. It's subversive."

Violently, he hurls the paper to the floor.

"I swear I didn't interpret it that way," the prisoner says. She tries to make her voice sound conciliatory. "I interpreted it as a metaphor. A man speaks to his son, telling him he has the courage to endure anything in order for that son to be happy." She raises her head nobly. "I would do the same." Then she looks into the eyes of the man standing before her, as if she could understand something very profound beneath that fierce gaze. "And I'm sure you would do it, too."

"I," says the Shark, pounding his chest, "I would die for a son. But the bastard who wrote this . . ."

"Forget about who wrote it for now; it's not so important. I hung it up because I liked the part about the little doves. And the fact that he was writing to his son. That's why I think I hung it up, because I would like to write to my daughter, too."

With relief, she notes that the traces of anger are vanishing from the Shark's face. But she doesn't hang the poem back on the wall. As she continues talking about her daughter and the little doves, she picks the paper up from the floor, discreetly smoothing it out, and throws it into the trash.

Nine

The newspaper article barely occupies a six-inch column. Diana, in bed, her back well-supported by two pillows, ritually reading the paper while drinking *mate*, is about to discover it, inconspicuous, on the police report page: *That's the disturbing part* (she had written), *that we keep up with our own rituals and even feel a certain pleasure in doing so, that I'm still able to stop to test the exact temperature of the water, to slowly pour the first stream; that as I patiently wait for the* mate *to brew, I open my front door and bring in the paper. And then, like someone who's organizing a little party, I arrange two pillows and climb back into bed to read while I have my* mate. *This little act – hasn't it always been a sign of order on a small scale? Later on, the day may fatally come undone, may break me into pieces, and I may end up exhausted, at the brink of chaos, with a vague feeling of failure, but this first ritual, so neatly sequenced, hasn't it always woven itself into a refuge? The suspicion that the day might still spin out into happiness? That, precisely, is the disturbing part: that now, too, performing this simple habit, I can still see, like a breath of air, what remains of a promise: the day isn't contaminated yet, Diana. Why couldn't it be possible that today, just today, things might not go all to hell and your little world might float calmly, pleasantly, towards . . . ? Which doesn't keep me from feeling, deep in my gut,* that lurking behind any bit of news, death might jump out and startle me.

But this time it doesn't startle her. In a sense she's been waiting for it for a month. Ever since that quick conversation with Professor Ordaz at the bus stop.

It states simply that in a confrontation with the Armed Forces and in the presence of his ten-year-old daughter, Montonero leader Fernando Kosac was killed. She covers her face with her hands, but Violeta's horrified eyes follow her in the uneasy darkness: they are focusing on her father's assassins, one after another. His body is still there, even though she has squeezed her eyes shut behind her hands. The bullet-ridden body of a man who was beautiful. And his transparent gaze – how does someone look one second before turning into a dead man? – like the only complete memory she has of him, a happy, summer night in 1962.

Although it might not be a single memory, but rather two, because if I try to tie the loose ends, the timing is off; it's not possible those two events happened on the same night or even that they happened at all. But that's how it was for me: everything happened on a single night, the luminous night of MAR's victory, not the planet but the Movement of the Armed Revolution, yet it bore the name it deserved, and for the first time, it had won – the left had won – the election in the College of Physical Sciences, which was why we danced that night at the yet-to-be-established university campus or at the old college in the District of Las Luces. It's all hazy in my memory and yet it all glows with its own light. We danced until our hearts were about to leap from our chests, to the rhythm of Carlos Puebla's songs, my God, all those names, all those words seem to have meaning: MAR, Puebla, and the vital act of moving our bodies with the animal happiness of our eighteen years also had a meaning; it formed a single, inseparable whole with that other happiness, the happiness of that Cuban music, which at the same time was a slap in the face to those who wanted to put a halt to history: And here is where they tried / to feign democracy /

while still in misery / the Cuban people died / And in this brutal hell / where robbery was the rule / they kept on being cruel / until they met Fidel. *Life was an explosion, a crazy Caribbean rhythm; everyone danced and so did I, to the beat of the rumba because I, too, loved shouting to the four winds* The game's over / the Comandante has arrived and called a halt, *although a certain incorrigible place inside me insisted on wondering if it was really true, if in these Southern lands the game would ever be over, and if this victory by a single student union was worth making such a fuss over, which was why, at some point, I stopped dancing and started looking with nostalgia and love – love for what is beautiful and well-placed in the world – at the boy with transparent, grey eyes and the young, olive-skinned woman with coppery hair. They look so intact, so lovely, so made for the rumba and for this time of revolution that just looking at them makes me feel exultant, and at the same time, inexplicably sad, as if I already know that this summer night and this party won't last forever. Then the boy with grey eyes looks at me with his transparent gaze. Perhaps it's just pity or perplexity. But I feel protected by that glance: even sad people and poets and those who can't find their place in the world will have a place in this world we are forging, that glance seems to be saying. Even though in another, unlikely corner of that same night, we're in Retiro Park celebrating the MAR victory between the roller coaster and the Ferris wheel, and I'm more or less alone and a little bit out of place, staring at those young activists as they turn around and around on the Ferris wheel, singing a song that goes* palo bonito, palo-é, *and wondering if I'm in this park just out of solidarity and if this staring makes any sense, just staring at the Ferris wheel turning. Then the boy with grey eyes, who has no doubt noticed my loneliness and wants to stop it, comes over to me in the startlingly splendorous night and miraculously speaks to me of Chekhov, of the delicate and persistent tragedy that always lies beneath Chekhov's everyday tales. And I feel there's a place in the world for me, after all.*

◆

"Was that the last time you saw him?" Garita asks.

"Why is that important?" Diana says.

"I mean," Garita says. "Because you don't talk much about the dead man in that part. You talk more about yourself. I'd like to know something important about the character."

Diana shrugs.

"I saw him again," she says. "But that's not what I want to tell."

"Pity," Garita says. "Because I have the impression that the heart of the matter always lies in the things you don't want to tell. Was it before or after Chekhov?"

"After," Diana says.

◆

Cold, grey eyes looking at her across the table at Café Tiziano. She, feeling proud because before coming in she had bought a yellow-leafed notebook – is this her fifth or sixth time as courier of the Czar's Mail? – and had resolved, by the time the awaited one arrived (she's always late) to come up with a suitable name for the dark-skinned girl with high cheekbones. She thought of "Leonora," and slowly, like someone determined to complete an assignment, wrote on the first page of the notebook: "The Story of Leonora and." She was about to begin writing her own name when she raised her eyes and noticed a change. The person coming towards her table was not Leonora, but a man, lovely, too, in his own way, but someone she didn't recognize until he stood next to her. Something's happened to Leonora, she thought. But the man (whom Diana decided to call Fernando), sat down next to her and said dryly:

"Leonora didn't come because she had something urgent to do."

Dark suit, silk tie. His expression isn't the one Diana recalls. Metallic and intimidating. He hands her some papers.

"You need to give these to Ordaz before tomorrow at noon," he says, like someone issuing military orders.

Diana feels slightly annoyed: this doesn't have much to do with Castor and Pollux. *Death changes people*, she thinks as they discuss banalities, two educated people exchanging opinions about the weather and pollution. *Contact with death changes people*. She makes an effort to shake off this thought and follow the story that he (perhaps so that her task won't seem like a low-level war mission, or perhaps moved by a mechanism like the one that made him approach her to talk about Chekhov on that splendorous night) is telling her now. A stopwatch. He's talking (since when?) about an excellent stopwatch that has stopped working; he left it at the Lutz Ferrando Jewellers three days before he and Leonora had to flee. The receipt was in their apartment, but of course the military had taken it away together with the books – a suggestive look – five leather-bound volumes of *Das Kapital*, irreplaceable, needless to say. He absolutely needed that stopwatch (there was a fleeting pause during which Diana could imagine operations timed by stopwatch that became embroiled in her mind with the adventure and the dream).

"So I waited a week and finally I went to Lutz Ferrando. I stared hard at the clerk and said, 'I left a stopwatch here to be fixed on such-and-such a day, but I've lost the receipt.' The girl flipped through a file box and gave me a terrified look. 'We can't give it to you,' she said, 'we can't give it to you.' I stared at her, hard, and backed away, very slowly, without taking my eyes off her. She was frightened, but she didn't dare move." He laughed. "She must've thought I was about to pull out a Ballester-Molina right then and there and blow her away."

Diana observes the cold eyes watching her without condescension and thinks, yes the girl must have been scared out of her mind, and what the hell does that have to do with the five leather-bound volumes of *Das Kapital*. She nimbly manages to suppress a flash, one that now, five years later, she suppresses again: she brushes the hair from her forehead like someone who's decided to cleanse her thoughts of all impurities.

"Not every part of reality is significant," she tells Garita. "Or else, to make it all significant, you'd need to keep so many facts in mind that, instead of a tale, you'd have to retell life itself." She shrugs. "Besides, this isn't Fernando's story, it's Leonora's."

And, like a delayed realization, she thinks it's lucky that Fernando learned so quickly not to feel pity. Because that icy, implacable expression – her last memory of him – must have been the one with which he faced his murderers before he died.

◆

The formed image doesn't entirely match the facts. It's only logical: it's constructed from data in the newspaper, and the newspaper only tells part of the truth. It's true that the shootout took place in front of Violeta. For nearly a month she hadn't been away from her father, except for the few nights when it was his turn to go out looking for supplies (on other occasions, it was Toña's turn, but Toña had left without a word two days before the men arrived, and then they were alone and her daddy didn't leave her side, not even for one minute). When he went out, she sat on the floor near the door, listening to the footsteps in the street, saying, "Guardian Angel, make him come back," just as her mommy had taught her to say every time she felt afraid. "There is no guardian angel," her daddy would say, "just men and women and kids. That's why we have to fight: to build a better world for everybody here on earth." What her daddy said was nice, but her mommy knew how to make things easier. She said that even though they didn't believe in God, her Guardian Angel was a good thing and she could call on him without any problem whenever she was afraid, because he would protect her, just like the fairies in fairy tales. "If you want stories, I've got stories," her daddy said, and when she went to bed, he came and sat down beside her with a book and read her a story. Especially "The Pretty Little House," which was in the book of Russian stories and was the one she liked best.

"Who owns this pretty little house? Who lives in it?"

"I, I, the Hungry Little Fly," she replied before her daddy had time to read it. And even though it was obvious (and her daddy told her so) that he didn't need to read it to her because she already knew it by heart, every night she asked for that story and nothing else, as if listening to it, exactly the same way again and again, might create a halo of security around her, a refuge, something that would remain unchanged even if they had to run from one house to another, always sleeping in different beds and among different people, and even though many times her mommy and daddy wouldn't be there and she would have to pray, against her daddy's wishes, "Guardian Angel, make them come back," just as her mommy had taught her. But that was before, when her mommy and daddy told her about a better world they were building for children like her, and in all the houses where they had lived, there was someone who sang or played the guitar, and changing her last name in order to go to school was like a game; besides, there always was a teacher her mommy could tell the secret to, and that teacher would love her more than the others and would make things easier for her. Later on, nobody sang or played the guitar or told her about her Guardian Angel anymore, and she didn't know why, but everything scared her and her daddy didn't tell her stories. Now he did again, sometimes. Now that the two of them were hiding in this house with Toña because they had taken her mommy away and she might never see her again, and Toña's husband, too; now she asked for Russian stories every night, and even though he didn't have the book and said she was too big for stories, he tried to remember and he repeated them to her almost word for word (especially for the last two days, when Toña went away too and her daddy never left her side, not even to get supplies), the one about the grandfather who planted a hare, and the one about Czarina Frog, and especially the one about the pretty little house, the one she liked best.

111

In that respect, at least, the newspaper had told the truth. They were never apart, so when the men came and surrounded the house, Violeta was there. And she also was there during the shootout. What wasn't true was that he died in the confrontation. It couldn't even be proved that something resembling the word "confrontation" had taken place, although it wouldn't be easy to describe it with another name. What can one call the action produced by fifteen men with machine guns, surrounding the front of a house and stationed on the roofs of neighbouring houses, and a tired man who defends himself against the shooting from behind a window, with his daughter a few steps away, crying from underneath a table, "Daddy, I don't want you to die"?

◆

"There's a glimmer of hope." This sentence, which evokes the image of an ancient doctor unburdening himself to the dying man's wife in an old black and white movie, will be the last one Diana will remember spoken by Professor Ordaz. Not because she didn't see him again. Several more times, like today getting off the number 128 bus to go to the Bechofen woman's place, she would see him in the distance, always with that vaguely heroic appearance she so admired when she was ten. But she would no longer go running to him as she does on this November afternoon, with Violeta's terrified expression still fixed in her mind.

"Have you heard anything?" she asks anxiously.

"There's a glimmer of hope."

Diana feels a certain uneasiness, not so much on account of the word hope (pathetically naïve coming from a man like him) but because of his tone. An optimistic tone, almost enthusiastic. Yes, she'd seen hopeful men and women, especially in April and May and June, when it was still hard to accept that the realm of possibility had overflowed its borders. *My son will come back; he's only seventeen. My brother is a union official; my granddaughter is pregnant,* as though a certain elemental logic still controlled the facts. But it was an increasingly fading hope because the shreds of horror were taking on an impossible shape, and then darkly they began to accept the fact that any nightmare could come true. For that reason, Diana thought the Professor's optimistic tone seemed out of place, even repulsive.

"About Violeta, I mean. If you've heard anything about Violeta. Today I read in the paper that Fernando . . ."

The Professor silences her with his usual gesture.

"Violeta is with us," he whispers into Diana's ear. "They called us at dawn to come downstairs, and they threw her out of a car. She was a little bit drugged, poor thing."

"But how is she now?" asks Diana, barely containing a sudden impulse to kick the Professor in the balls.

"Just fine," the Professor says.

Diana quickly glances at his fly.

"Excuse me, I have to go," she says quickly. "Someone's waiting for me."

And she walks away from the Professor with the disagreeable feeling that she's about to throw up.

◆

Besides being tired, he's also perplexed: barricaded behind the window, surrounded by men who must have been aiming at the patio from the rooftops and who shone reflectors on the house from the front, he couldn't understand why they hadn't shot their way in through the doors. He was surrounded, the voice over the loudspeaker had said, there was no way out. But the discharge that came later seemed intended not so much to kill him as to communicate a message: we can wipe you out whenever we feel like it. He responded by shooting.

"We know about your daughter," the voice said, and he was surprised at the intimacy of the tone. "We'll give you time to send her out." Then it added, "We have her mother."

"*Dead*," he said to himself and began shooting again.

Machine gun fired replied.

"It's in your hands," the voice said. "Your daughter's life. In your hands."

More shooting.

Violeta's sobs, muffled by the table, reached him from behind. *Mommy*, he heard through her sobs, and at the same time something about his wife pronounced over the loudspeaker. Something he didn't quite hear or that he thought he had misheard.

He turned his head, imagining Violeta's crouched body, her terrified eyes opened wide. She was no longer crying.

"Don't shoot," he said after a long silence. "Violeta's coming out."

He convinced her. With the voice he used to tell her Russian stories and with a promise he couldn't make himself believe: "You're going to see your mommy," and he kissed her goodbye. He thought that it was strange, saying goodbye forever. Strange, this dying business.

He saw her go out, slow and dishevelled, her long hair falling over her face like when she just woke up and climbed into his bed; he imagined machine guns silently aimed at her from the shadows. Then he didn't see her anymore; he had no time. Now the bullets broke the windows and penetrated the walls. The voice over the loudspeaker also penetrated the walls, only they were distorted by the din. He shot furiously at that voice.

Until something happened. It might have been because when he stopped shooting for a moment, he finally heard what the voice on the loudspeaker was saying. Perhaps he tried to give himself an opportunity to prove it was a lie and for that reason he stopped shooting. Or it might have been because, strangely, he envisioned himself in Higueras, in someone else's story that he had dreamed of so often – *Don't shoot, I'm Che Guevara* – the man with the naked torso and the face of Christ believing that something in those words would stay the hand of the men aiming at

114

him, or in spite of everything, trusting in his seed and in the unconquerable lineage of the New Man.

"Don't shoot. I'm coming out," was heard by those outside, a voice that Violeta would hear in dreams many years later.

He appeared at the door. His shoulder was wounded and he was unarmed. He didn't look at them with the icy expression that Diana Glass would redeemingly give him. Nor with the transparent gaze with which he had approached a lonely teenage girl on a night of voluptuous Cuban music to talk to her of Chekhov.

It was a new situation, so his expression – which tried to discern the man with the loudspeaker from all the other – was a new expression.

"Daddy," said Violeta.

"Fire," said the Shark.

◆

What isn't true is that he died at that moment, as the newspaper article suggested. And it also isn't true what they told Violeta a month later, by a swimming pool with turquoise water in the shade of a laurel tree: that her daddy died a month later, peacefully and in her mommy's arms; that her mommy had promised him that she would take good care of her, of Violeta, and she told him she loved him very much and would never forget him. And that she closed his grey eyes.

False. She didn't close his eyes, and he didn't die in her arms, but it is true that the meeting took place. In an ambulance, bleeding to death but still conscious, he was taken to the infirmary at the School; the person who accompanied him, seated next to the stretcher and speaking to him, was the Shark. It was also the Shark who led the prisoner from her flowery little cell – where she passionately wrote the story of the revolutionary struggle – to the place where her husband lay.

"I kept my end of the deal," he told her before opening the infirmary door. "Violeta is safe."

115

And he left them alone.

What happened at that meeting isn't easy to prove, but that's not important: it has already been established that absolute truth does not exist. Besides, how much weight would a look of reproach or confusion or hatred have (assuming it could even be produced), coming from someone who's about to die? Someone who's about to die is already, to a certain extent, dead. The little disarticulation between the point when he might ask the prisoner why she looks so fit and why the officer who directed the operation that killed him treats her with such respect, and that other point at which all rancour and all desire and all tiny palpitations disappear, that disarticulation is so insignificant as to be beneath consideration. She, the survivor, needs only to exercise her will. To bear the dying man's gaze, to repeat to herself again and again: this is the exact moment to show strength because if she cries out – but she doesn't even consider it; the secret is not even to wonder if it's still possible for her to cry out, if rebelling is still possible – if right now she were to shout you bastards, you've destroyed him, you're destroying all of us, then her own life would be lost, and who would benefit from that?

Aside from these exercises, the rest is simple. Only God will remain a witness of this encounter, and her God is as practical as she is. He reasons that saving oneself is a sine qua non. Besides, he must be Divinely Happy to have recovered her to His bosom: the prisoner prays to Him every morning and every night, and He redeems her of all suffering, He protects her from the screams of horror that she hears from the attic. What could she do (He asks her) for those who are screaming, what could she do for the man with the bullet-riddled chest who is staring at her, who still stares at her? God has absolved her; she can live in peace. The only truth is life. The one who's listening from behind the infirmary door to make sure he won't be betrayed – he kept his part of the deal and expects loyalty – the one who perhaps is listening is alive. On the other hand, the one who's still staring at her is about to die. When they take him away, when his grey gaze disappears, the prisoner will be the sole owner of this little episode. Like a treasure, Violeta can keep what she will hear beside the turquoise swimming pool, beneath the laurel tree. And I will hear the description of a scene, that, when you think about it, might not be so far from the truth: that he died at the prisoner's side, that she managed to tell him that Violeta was safe and he to tell her that the units were reorganizing and when they were strong again, they would undertake the definitive battle against the enemies of the people. To the final victory.

"In the end, he died with his faith," she will tell me. Riddled with bullets from the gunfight and trusting fully in the triumph of the revolution.

"Leonora always did like Russian films," Diana will say.

Ten

She's sitting on the bed, alert to the sound of footsteps. She doesn't appear calm, but it's not the time of day that's perturbing her: at this point she knows perfectly well that even in the attic, midnight is a time of activity, and not just on Wednesdays, when they take away some of the kidnapped victims to make room for new ones and there's general unrest; any other night of the week one can hear footsteps, keys in locks, the distant shout of a number, and then more steps retracing their path, dragging a body. "For God's sake, not again, I can't take it anymore!" she heard a woman scream barely half an hour ago. And so it's not the nocturnal footsteps that alarm her, but rather the fact that this time, the footsteps are approaching her door.

She turned in her report on the Organization's history a week ago, and she wonders if the Admiral will be so detail-minded as to note that she's no longer of any use to them. You can't keep collecting live prisoners forever, the Shark had explained to her on one of those confidential afternoons following the death of her husband. And, scientifically speaking, the prisoner can't help but agree. Physical space is limited: if people come in, people must go out: it's crystal clear, and people must come in because subversion has to be eliminated down to its most infinitesimal elements. "Because wherever a seed remains, no matter how small," the Shark had told her, "one day a forest will grow." The procedure is quite straightforward (he explained to her): they round up the prisoners for a relocation (sometimes telling them they're going to be set free), inject them with sedatives in order to avoid a commotion, tie their hands and feet together with wire and throw them into the river from a plane. Killing them beforehand would be a redundancy: fear and the water make it unnecessary. "Quick and easy," the Shark said. "You can't keep collecting live prisoners forever. There's still plenty left to eliminate if this is to become the Fatherland our leaders dreamed of." And so her heart beats out of control now that the footsteps have stopped outside her door.

There's a moment of silence. Then someone fiddles with the locks. The action lasts longer than usual, as though the person outside didn't know how to open the door or was very clumsy. The prisoner doesn't dare move: eyes fixed on the door, she waits for the stranger to enter.

◆

"Russian films?" Garita asks.

"*The Forty-First.* I especially remember *The Forty-First.* They were showing it in Cinema Roca, in a double bill with *The Cranes Are Flying.* The girl in *The Cranes Are Flying* looked like Leonora, or maybe she gave that impression; she had heroic qualities, Leonora, I mean: all the heroines looked like Leonora. Or vice versa. At the end of *The Cranes Are Flying,* the heroine was left alone, at a station or someplace with a lot of people, crying silently because he had died in the war. Leonora and I cried at the movies, too, but I don't know, it wasn't a sad kind of crying, I mean there was hope, for the girl or for the people at the station, I can't exactly remember, but it's just that there was some hope, as though everything were conspiring to tell us that war and death and injustice and all the miserable things they insisted on showing us would spill over into a time of happiness that it was our job to create."

◆

But the person at the door, holding something wrapped up in newspaper under his arm, is no stranger. It's the Shark.

"I came to toast with you," he says.

His voice drags, as if it were hard for him, after each syllable, to find the next one. Walking erect also seems to demand quite an effort of him. He stops next to the bed and solemnly unwraps the package.

Only when she sees the contents – a bottle of champagne and two paper cups – does the prisoner realize that the Shark is drunk. She has no experience with the effects of alcohol; she comes from a rational home where anything that might muddle clarity of mind was disdained, and from a Party for which the excesses of alcohol and sex were thought to smack of bourgeois culture. It's true that later on she took part in guitar fests with plenty of wine, but in those days everything seemed to form part of the same earthy festival: applauding Chacho Peñaloza, singing to the Tucumán moon, drinking (not the prisoner, no – she's never needed to get high on anything but life itself), or celebrating the death throes of imperialism. Wine hardly changed anything. Perhaps a bit more fervour, but how could anyone notice it at a time when fervour was the norm? *We were all a little drunk*, Diana wrote; *we all let ourselves get carried away in an inebriation of slogans, as though singing "I have faith that Chile will win" were an incantation that could cancel out death in the stadiums of Santiago, as if chanting "Viva Che Guevara!" would make him descend from the Sierra Maestra and diligently establish socialism in our own land.*

But the Shark's situation is something else. Now that she has him close at hand, the prisoner can detect his odour and the slight hesitation of his hand as he fills the two glasses. He hands her one.

"Today's my birthday," he tells her.

Birthdays were happy occasions. One more year meant growing closer to something mysterious, but desired. And then there were the gifts. I could draw a road map of the evolution of our souls by the gifts we exchanged. They were always books; we looked down on those girls who gave handkerchiefs or bracelets. When Leonora turned nine, I gave her The Tigers of Malaysia *and at sixteen* The Pedagogical Poem *by Matarenko (we were in our fourth year of Teachers' Prep School and blindly believed that a noble education would result in a noble humanity, but above all we believed, since we were going to be teachers, that we had no choice but to revolutionize teaching and revolutionize the world in the process, since nothing we did could ever be destined to fall into the void). After we turned seventeen – that time it was Juan Gelman's* Violin and Other Questions *– there were no more shared celebrations. Life began to lead us down twisted paths. But whenever that September day came along, I would say to myself: "Today is Leonora's birthday," and it was as if, somehow, we were still together.*

"Then I wish you a very happy birthday," the prisoner says enthusiastically, tapping her paper cup against the Shark's.

She takes a tiny sip, then rests the cup on the floor. When she raises her eyes, she notices that the Shark's are filled with tears.

"Excuse me," the Shark says. "It chokes me up to hear a woman say that to me. A woman like you, I mean."

The prisoner waits expectantly: this man seems about to fling open a dangerous door.

"Aren't you married?" she asks cautiously.

The Shark doesn't seem to have heard her. He starts to sit down on the edge of the bed. Yet, because he misses the mark, or because something has made him change his mind, he ends up on the floor. He balances the bottle very delicately. Then, with exquisite care, he places his glass beside the prisoner's.

"Didn't you celebrate with anyone?" asks the prisoner as though she had forgotten about her previous question.

121

The Shark looks at her, puzzled; he seems erratic.

"I was toasting at the canteen with the other guys," he says, finally. "Around here you celebrate as much as you can. If you don't, with all the shit you see in here, excuse my language, but you understand, I don't know, sometimes I think I can tell you anything and you'll understand."

"I try to understand," the prisoner says. She observes him very closely before going on, like someone walking through unknown terrain in the dark. "In the long run, you realize that everyone has his own truth."

The Shark shakes his head again and again.

"No, no, no. That's where the error lies," and he remains in suspense as if he suddenly couldn't remember where the error was. At last he downs the remainder of the contents of the glass in a single gulp and seems to wake up.

"There's only one truth. What happens is that some people . . ." He refills his glass. "Some people don't even realize that they're wrong; I'll grant you that much. Assholes who don't even know how to sing the whole national anthem and who look at you like they can't believe what . . ." He makes a gesture to fill the prisoner's glass, but she points to show him her glass is still full. He drinks. "We have to wipe them out anyway; we have to wipe out all the garbage that piled up in Argentina and as soon as possible, so it'll go back to being what it was. It's like a serious illness: you have to operate, with or without anesthesia, in order to save the organism. That's what those people out there don't understand. And when you bring them in, it's worse. They spit at you, they swear at you, they disrespect you, and I've had enough disrespect from . . ." He looks at her as if he were about to tell her something confidential. Finally, he empties his glass. "I'm not about to put up with disrespect from some Commie traitor to the Fatherland." He lifts his finger, like someone about to give a warning. "But I don't do it for pleasure, don't get me wrong; I do it out of duty. I tell myself, this is a mission you have to fulfill, Sharkey, this vagina, these nipples are your target; you have to rip these nails off because if you don't, the Fatherland will fall into foreign hands. I think of the flag fluttering against the sky and then . . . Once, in grade four, it was my turn to raise the flag, and I don't know, when I heard *Aurora* and saw it rising to the top because my hands were the ones making it rise, I don't know, maybe it was that day when I swore to myself that I would defend the Fatherland against anyone who attacked it. Those are ideals; without ideals, you're nobody; you should understand these things." He raises the glass to his mouth but realizes it's empty. He tries to refill it, but the bottle is empty, too; he casts a fleeting glance at the prisoner's glass. "The worst ones aren't those who scream," he says abruptly, "or even the ones who insult you; the worst ones are those who stare at you silently. That's why the most convenient thing is to put the hood on them, but sometimes . . . You realize that they don't know anything and yet they believe they have the right to look at you that way. They're the ones who stay firm until the last minute; those are the real enemies, because those people think they own the truth. You've got to eliminate them without being disgusted. And without hatred, believe me. Sometimes I don't even feel like going; I feel kind of nauseous, I don't know, and yet the Falcon gives the order, and there I am, fulfilling my duty. Do you get what I mean? This isn't pleasant work. Necessary, yes, but not pleasant." He shrugs. "Other guys like it, I won't deny it, but not me. I go home tired, fed up with dealing with any problems. You know what my dream would be? A house with a bunch of kids begging me all together for a piggyback ride. Hey, hey, take it easy, one at a time, I'd tell them. But my wife doesn't want to, I don't know, she feels superior. When I get home, there she is with some novel or some magazine and she doesn't even bother to look at me. Superior to what, I want to know, you're the real reader, not her, it's so obvious, but you don't give me dirty looks; you respect me. What I'd love – these are just dreams, you see so much crap around here that if you don't dream a little, I don't know where we'd end up – I'd love to go home at night to someone like you and be able to forget my work a little, and for you to stroke my head, like that, like that, it feels so peaceful that way, life seems so pleasant; I think I'm falling asleep."

◆

But *The Forty-First* was something else, she says; it showed a zone of shadows, an ambiguous game that made being a revolutionary more complex, and also more heroic. I can imagine Garita's face as he listens to her: he doesn't believe her story very much; that is, he thinks she's hiding something from him – or from herself. Each time she harps on her famous "being a revolutionary" theme (he tells me after everyone's gone home and he can just be himself) or enthusiastically becomes absorbed by the novels they used to read, the films they preferred, the garlands they didn't know how to make, I think she's putting off something that she herself doesn't recognize. Garita has taken this as a sort of detective novel plot: he wants to discover, at all costs, who the murderer is. And I? I want to discover *her*. Or discover myself? Something crystallized for me back in Vienna, before I came here, something that, with this death all around, is fighting to leap out bit by bit. What's that old woman hiding, as she stirs stew in her kitchen and eavesdrops on other people's stories? Sometimes I imagine her asking herself something like that and I feel flattered. But maybe I'm mistaken: maybe she doesn't even think about me because she's so involved with herself. Now she's explaining that the woman – tall and blonde, with short hair, that's how she remembers her – was fighting for Communism, and he – she thinks he was blond, too, although she can't say for sure – was a White Russian. He was fighting against the revolution. He's been taken prisoner by the revolutionaries and the one assigned to watch him is the blonde woman. They're in an isolated place, a beach, she thinks, because she remembers the sea. It's all wonderfully harmonious, she says, their blue eyes, the golden sand, the solitude, the sea. They fall in love as people do sometimes, not just in movies. It's a strange thing, love, and she wanders off, just as she sometimes wanders off when she can forget about the stone wall she's built around herself. It's interesting to observe her at times like these: she sounds confused, although there's a certain coherence beneath it all, more meaningful than what she's struggling to illustrate when she talks about her story. Now she's forgotten about it; she's lost in the vicissitudes of love: the unlikelihood that two people who love one another would meet, she says, the fortuitous circumstances of their meeting. The revolutionary and her prisoner love each other madly, she says, but also desperately, because they both know, or she knows – because the cause that really matters to the viewer, the noble cause, open to the future, is her cause, too – that choosing this passion, this joy, means betraying the hopes of others. And her own hope, the dream that defines the blonde woman as a human being? she wonders.

The water has begun to boil. Time to take out the codfish and put the pot with the garlic on the stove. It's important to have the pieces of leek and potato ready. I savour the aroma that gently begins to fill the room and which will reach them like a gift, or the promise of a gift, through the half-open door behind which the prisoner is fleeing; I understand that a comrade has found a small boat for him. She watches him from the shore, observes how he fades into the distance. Then, with tear-filled eyes but with a firm pulse, she aims her rifle. A revolution that will turn the century around is at stake. The Russian woman weeps and everyone in the theatre weeps along with her, she says. There's a moment of stillness, a moment when everything is possible. Then, inevitably, the Russian woman fires.

A discussion ensues. Is the ending realistic? Is it ethical? What does ethical mean? The only ethical choice – her tone is categorical – was to choose the transcendental cause, in this case, the cause of an entire people.

I put the fried garlic in the grinder, and the pieces of leek and potato into the pot, together with the codfish. It needs to simmer. I wonder if the fact that her heroine fired the vindicating bullet so glibly hasn't harmed her a little, if it hasn't addled her brain like the novels of chivalry addled poor Alonso Quijano's. Perhaps she could have used a little more uncertainty, a brief freeze-frame one second before the shot rings out (I add the water from the codfish, cover it, and let it simmer, time to crush the garlic), at the end of the film when the main character is still aiming and weeping. So that she might feel in her own bones the vertigo of suspecting that one can be vulnerable to slipping on many paving stones on the road to victory and death. At any rate, let us leave the kettle on a slow flame. In an hour the fish stew will be ready.

◆

It was strange to hear him say that, the prisoner would tell me, because she had never stroked his head. She had simply watched him while, sitting on the floor, he talked and talked, at first with his eyes glued to the bottle, then resting his cheek on the edge of the bed, until gradually he fell asleep. And it wasn't that she didn't feel like stroking it, because she had a soft spot for scrappy men who revealed their vulnerability to her. It wasn't the first time this had happened (she would tell me); more than one little rooster had shown her his torn feathers, and that made her feel pleasure as well as pride. And so her natural impulse had really been to stroke his head as soon as he rested his cheek on the bed and mentioned his wife, only he had taken her by surprise with the business of "stroking my head like that," as if just imagining the situation were enough, or as if he wouldn't allow himself such liberties. Or as if he wouldn't allow her to take them, and that's what really made her hesitate. And so she held back the impulse, resigning herself to listening to his monologue, growing ever more muffled, with quiet hands, until he fell asleep and she, too, fell asleep at last. "That was the first night we slept together," she told me by way of finishing.

"Yes, she had a sense of humour," Diana would comment darkly. "It always was one of the traits we shared, humour."

She was wrong. The prisoner lacks that fierce and pitiless, but at the same time impartial and all-comprehending, quality that is humour. She can understand, and even conceive of, something amusing, but she will lack even the slightest trace of an internal chuckle as she tells me how the Shark fell asleep, while, at the same time, she rocks the baby. One can't even be sure that the phrase, "That was the first night we slept together" contains a nuance of humour. She might have said it with a touch of romanticism, alluding to a ritual that began under precarious, but longed-for conditions, just as Swann named the cattleyas. Or simply pointing out an objective fact: *The first time we slept together.* An isolated event, the mere product of a drunken binge that dulled inhibitions, allowing the Shark to do what he wanted to do: rest his head near the prisoner's body and sleep. A small parenthesis that ends in the morning, no sooner than the two of them open their eyes. There's a brief apology on the part of the Shark and a broad, hospitable smile on the part of the prisoner. But undoubtedly some sediment of tenderness remains in both of them, a certain delicate net that is already spinning a love story.

Eleven

A good Jewish husband like yours, the mother told my mother (Diana said), a husband who comes home at night carrying a package. And the other woman confessed to her (my mother told me) how she liked watching my father from the window every night at dusk, when he would appear on Cangallo on the way to my house, whistling offhandedly. Or maybe she didn't say that last part, maybe I'm imagining him, distracted as usual, whistling *Mano a mano* or one of those little Creole waltzes that he danced to so well as he passed beneath Señora Ordaz's window carrying something wrapped in pristine white paper which the woman observing him (although she didn't say this to my mother) must have dreamed was happiness. And maybe she wasn't mistaken: that's where the little nocturnal feast was contained: sweet-and-sour gherkins, a pickled herring, a piece of *Apfelstrudel*, a miraculous gadget for shelling peas, offered by a street vendor whose charms he hadn't been able to resist, an object that lit up the night and made it special – so that, seen from a distance, what the mother told my mother wasn't so ridiculous, my mother explained, without concealing her pride, although at the time, I listened with some skepticism since, even more than the little nightly ceremony in white wrapping paper, I longed for a father who could speak eloquently about public education and pronounce the words "great leaders" or "singular hero" as easily as if he were saying *pletzlach* with onions, and therefore I couldn't see the advantage of having a good Jewish husband like hers, as the mother said to my mother and my mother told me. And since we both know, dear lady, that by now that's impossible, what I ask God is that one day Leonora, when she's grown, might have a husband like that, a good Jewish husband who worries about the household and is married to her and not to politics, the mother said to my mother.

◆

And on this pleasant December afternoon, she feels like God has heard her. It's true the man she's spiritedly chatting with beneath the laurel tree, a few steps away from the kidney-shaped swimming pool with its turquoise water, this very polite young man, doesn't resemble the good Jewish husband she dreamed of for her daughter so many years ago, but it's equally true that life has taught her not to trust even Jewish husbands. Her son-in-law, may he rest in God's holy glory in spite of everything, that gentle, beautiful man whom she had met in his sailor's uniform and about whom she had thought, "At last someone's come along to rein in my only daughter's impossible character," turned out to be even more impossible than she; no wonder he ended up shot full of holes while her daughter – it seems like a dream! – now stands in the turquoise water hugging Violeta over and over as if neither one of them can believe how lucky they are to be together again. And so, although the young man she's talking to doesn't resemble the good Jewish husband with the white paper-wrapped package, you can see right away that he's a well-bred person with a good head on his shoulders; he's talking to her about these youngsters who have been deluded by foreign lies, about the harsh corrective measures that often must be taken, and she agrees with him entirely.

Her own husband – always so demanding – has pondered this young man's propriety and must understand why. After the early morning call when he heard his daughter's voice for the first time on the telephone – "I'm at the School and I'm all right" – he told her she'd said, "and from now on everything depends on me. And on you. I'm going to hand the phone over to someone else now." After that early morning, her husband spoke to this very nice young man several more times. And not just with him, he explained, but also with others who are much higher up. He hasn't given her any other details, nor has she tried to find out; political intrigue has never interested her.

What does interest her is that she owes this young man the first bit of happiness she's had in these times. She'll never forget the ring of the telephone at three AM, followed by her husband's laconic explanation: "It was the Captain. He said to go downstairs; they're going to hand something to us from a passing car." Nor will she forget waiting, the two of them, exhausted in the silent night, or the Ford Falcon skidding as it turned the corner of Salguero and barely slowed down in front of the house in order to toss out a bundle that she, at first, as though her worst nightmares could become reality, thought was her daughter's corpse. But no, it was her only granddaughter, drugged with tranquilizers but in one piece, her blonde hair all dishevelled, her sobbing hardly audible.

Besides, the young man has fulfilled his promise. All this is happening as planned. Two men in a car came to pick them up at the arranged time and brought them to this lovely country house. Except for the dark, newspaper-lined glasses he put on both of them, everything has worked out completely normally. *But why the little one?* she wanted to ask, and she might even have added, and *why me, when I'm eternally grateful to you and will pray every night for the salvation of your souls,* but studying the two men's faces a little, she decided not to say anything. It seemed strange to her, she can't deny it, to be travelling blindly in a car in the company of two strangers, going who-knows-where, feeling Violeta's hand – the only thing familiar – as it tightly squeezed her own and wondering if she was feeling just as strange, although maybe not, she's experienced so many things in her ten years of life: she watched her father get shot to death hardly three weeks ago, although she never spoke of that. Señora Ordaz found out only from the newspaper article and now from what she half-hears her daughter saying to Violeta in the water, that Daddy died in my arms, but first he told me he loved us both very much and he asked me to take care of you, and meanwhile the young man clears his throat, momentarily distant from the conversation.

And now she's sitting in the cool shade of the laurel tree, chatting with this well-mannered young man and observing the scene that she most longed for in these troubled days: her grand-daughter, smiling for the first time since that dawn, with her arm around the waist of her daughter, who's now floating on her back, leading her, now making a tunnel between her legs for Violeta to swim through, plunging into the water and emerging, her head thrown backwards, her thick hair dripping, her radiant face to the sky, so beautiful in that bathing suit with its tiny flowers (too feminine, she had thought, and involuntarily it had occurred to her that its owner must have been one of those women who baked biscuits and polished her nails light pink. What could she have done to make her bathing suit end up here, she thought, shaking her head vigorously to chase away the disturbing thought. Today was a happy morning; for the first time, they'd removed the cuff from her leg and for the first time, she was going to see her daughter. She thought that the Shark, who stood beside her waiting for her to choose a bathing suit, was growing impatient. "That one you've got in your hand, I'm sure it'll fit you very well," he said. "Do you think so?" the prisoner asked, a little coquettishly. "Then that's that – I'll take it"), so feminine, which proves she's changing, and the man who's been chatting with her and who now stands up and walks over to the swimming pool must have had a lot to do with that change.

Gallantly he extends his hand to help the woman in the daintily flowered bathing suit exit the pool; then he lifts up the little girl and kisses her on the cheeks. The picture is so touching that it makes her eyes grow moist. If it weren't for the four armed men who, from a few feet away from the pool, observe the protagonists' every movement, she would even dare say this is as beautiful as a dream.

◆

Ironic, she finally said, because Fernando was sort of Jewish, at least on his father's side. But the world isn't as well-ordered as Señora Ordaz thought. I'm glad you recognize that occasionally, Garita said. They never stop fighting, the Bechofen woman observed as she carefully added three spoonfuls of paprika, one of tomato paste, and a cup of water to the pot where the onion was browning; that seems to be the only incentive those two find for coming to these gatherings. Aside from my presence, I hope. And she smiled as she stirred the contents of the pot; she was pleased that they no longer caused her distress: she dedicated herself to them with real scientific interest, although this time something of uncertain origin had drawn her attention, something she couldn't figure out. She tossed the pieces of chicken into the pot.

I think you have the wrong idea about me, Diana said in a less belligerent tone than usual (maybe she's figured out that I'm listening to her from behind the kitchen door, the Bechofen woman thought, and she wants me to think she's more calm and collected than she really is.) I don't believe the world is well ordered, quite the contrary. Probably that's why I try to hold on to, I don't know, to recover what was once rational, what still retained a certain order.

Pickled herring, the Bechofen woman thought abstractedly, realizing that what had caught her attention a few moments earlier was that unusual note in Diana Glass's speech, as if in spite of it all, something had come flooding out of her, little cataclysms that deformed the transparent structure she blindly insisted on building. Like this *páprikas csirke* that we'll eat later, gathered around the table, and which will temporarily make us rejoice and forget death. Little moments, harmonious or melancholy or absurd, that disappear as soon as you remove them from their isolation but which nonetheless remain there, so embedded in the story that discounting them as too trivial would mean telling a different story. Or telling a void. That's what she insists on not seeing, and I probably won't tell her because if she's going to learn it, she'll learn it all by herself.

Just a bit of help, she told herself, smiling again because what had just occurred to her wasn't an act of generosity but rather a little *mise-en-scène* that will place her momentarily in the foreground. She heard the echoes of a general argument, heard Garita's sarcastic voice: "I'd like to know what it is that once had a certain order," and Diana's words, slightly threatening.

"So you'd like to know what-it-is-that-once-had-a-certain-order," she said, menacing or stalling for time.

And before she could shape an explanation of whatever it was she was about to utter, the Bechofen woman opened the kitchen door, and relishing beforehand the restrained state of shock her words would produce, announced:

"Pickled herring."

◆

Making the most of the long summer afternoons, she goes out walking with the Shark. They don't have much in common to talk about, but they manage: they chat about Violeta, about the prisoner's mother (whom the Shark considers to be a very pleasant woman), or about general aspects of their work.

The work is hard, no doubt about it, Leonora (they now call each other by their first names); they might be hiding in a church, at a school; you can't make a single mistake because if you allow even one to escape, subversion will grow like a weed. The prisoner participates very little in these exchanges, but she can't help admitting that, strategically speaking, what the Shark says is true. It's inevitable: one thinks in strategic terms just as one thinks in mathematical terms, and the prisoner has always had great abstract reasoning ability, no wonder she studied physics. The secret lies in not thinking about flesh-and-blood bodies. Fortunately, most of those bodies belong to people she doesn't even know.

There are exceptions, of course: the girl with the freckled nose whose name she prefers not to remember. She had no breath left for screaming, the Shark said, trembling with rage during one of those rare moments when, out of a sense of powerlessness or because he expected her to provide an explanation of the incomprehensible, he referred to his work in concrete terms. I tried to find her most sensitive parts – delicately avoiding mentioning those parts – but she still pressed her lips together and stared at me, without saying a word. "What's her name?" the prisoner had asked, perhaps suspecting something, and once she heard the name, "I know her; you have to know how to treat her." Perhaps she remembered her as she was the first time she saw the prisoner: the tiny body, the freckled nose, the force with which she said, "to change the world" and "the enemies of the people." A child of the middle class, she remembered thinking at the time, recalling how she had asked her, "Did you run away from home?" "That's my business," the girl had replied arrogantly. She was eighteen years old and wanted to charge into action right away. She'd had to use her best persuasive technique in order to convince her that a well-placed little screw in the machinery of the revolutionary struggle was worth more than a wild teenager planting bombs willy-nilly. The time for romantic, anarchist suicides had passed, she told her, and now there are well-organized groups and hierarchies, and what the boss says goes. She noted the contemptuous scowl at the word "hierarchies" and had to employ all her powers of seduction and all her authority in order to dispel the bad impression. She convinced her so thoroughly that, while under her command, the girl was the most obedient and most disciplined of her soldiers.

"You'll be wasting your time," the Shark had told her. "I know what we're dealing with." But the prisoner insisted because she had always liked that girl and because she had faith. She saw her naked, bleeding from the mouth and genitals, her face unrecognizable. She gently called her name, like a caress. The blue eyes opened as if they were heavy, and at first it seemed they saw nothing or didn't comprehend what they were seeing. Then something ignited in those eyes, a spark of shock or of fright, something that made the prisoner want to get out of there, to flee that gaze forever. But she didn't leave. Naively, she made once last attempt to save that girl. In a persuasive tone they both recognized, she told her it was necessary to be very brave in order to admit one's own mistakes, that she had faith that the girl was brave enough, that she'd have the courage to accept the fact – just as she herself had done – that they'd chosen the wrong path, and besides, those men weren't what the girl thought, although they looked like the enemy, inside every one of them sparked a truth it was important to heed: that the girl was very young, she had her whole life ahead of her, that life is sacred, that God . . .

"You bitch, you traitor! Listening to you is much worse than the *picana*." And she didn't hear anymore because the Shark ordered them to take her out of there. "I told you she was a lost cause," he managed to mutter before she walked away. The prisoner tried not to think about the episode, and above all she tried not to imagine, that on Wednesday, among the bodies dragging chains was the girl, perhaps dreaming of freedom, perhaps guessing her fate, perhaps cursing Leonora. She tried not to imagine the tiny body tied with wire, flying from a plane towards the river, in an attempt to cancel out definitively what the prisoner, with true faith, had called sacred.

Other subjects they discuss include: the intense heat, the prisoner's old neighbourhood, the Shark's old neighbourhood, their few mutual acquaintances – Sixfingers, the Angel, the Doctor, some prisoners, a few guards – the last movie they saw in the projection room of the School, how the days were subtly growing shorter. Trivialities that nonetheless add a pleasant touch to those walks on the long, summer afternoons.

♦

Pickled herring, the Bechofen woman said, as she stood contentedly at the kitchen door, contemplating the brief, enchanted interlude that her words had created. She enjoyed these little surprises or states of ambiguity, where the receiver must decide if he's facing an enigmatic lesson that he needs to decipher in order to achieve wisdom or a bad joke by an old eccentric. It's the only thing I can do for them, she thought. Prepare them for the unexpected. She glanced a little sadly at her hand with its tiny age spots. Although you can never be altogether prepared, she said to herself. She nodded slightly and returned to the kitchen.

Twelve

One afternoon in the middle of March, four months before the prisoner is released, the Falcon suddenly enters her cubicle. She puts herself on alert. The Falcon's visits always put her on alert. Not because he doesn't respect her; according to what the prisoner has observed, by now he's already realized that she isn't as easily seduced as some others; it's just that he can't reconcile himself to not sleeping with her. This time, however, the slightly lewd look he usually gives the prisoner has been relegated to second place. He has something important to communicate to her.

"You're going to see an acquaintance," he says.

This news doesn't make the prisoner happy. A week ago, he had brought in another acquaintance: her old classmate from the College of Sciences who had pointed her out on Calle Montes de Oca. It wasn't the first time she had seen him, but this time he had come to make her a concrete proposal. "The Falcon says you're someone that can be reasoned with," he had told her, inviting her to join the *staff*. And that was precisely what the prisoner needed: action. She had always had a clear mission in life; even two months before: while she was passionately and systematically recording the Organization's history, she had repeated to herself again and again: "The Admiral is going to be impressed with me: he can't even imagine the kind of report I'm writing," and she felt she was fulfilling a mission. But lately she'd only been performing isolated tasks: talking to some prisoner, expressing her opinion of some political event, doing the occasional translation from English. The rest of the time, she floated in empty space with no other consolation than the promise of seeing her daughter again, her outings with the Shark, and God's sanctuary. But it wasn't so simple: in order to act, she needed to be convinced. And what her visitor had proposed didn't convince her: marking people for death just like that, for example, simply wasn't something she did.

And so the Falcon's words didn't make her happy. "You're going to see an acquaintance."

He speaks, then pauses a bit theatrically. At last he continues:

"Someone at a high level, like you." He fixes his gaze on the prisoner with a mixture of seduction and intimidation. "The Admiral has high hopes for this meeting," he says. "He's sure something worthwhile will come of it."

A few minutes later, the prisoner, without much hope, follows him down a corridor.

They stop in front of a door. The Falcon signals to the guard on duty. The man pulls out a set of keys, chooses one, and turns it twice in the lock. But the one in charge of opening the door is the Falcon, as though this moment of supreme authority that suddenly and unavoidably exposes the presumed occupant to the eyes of others, belongs to him.

The prisoner looks inside and can't help crying out. It's a cry of surprise, but also – and especially – a cry of joy. Seated at a small table, with that slightly ironic, calm expression she knows so well, regarding her with unabashed emotion, is the Thrush.

◆

It's raining the Friday night of her departure. That's why, on the fourth floor (by elevator) of the house in Almagro, only a few members of Garita's workshop have gathered. Diana Glass is there: inexplicably, she's been coming every Friday for eight months now to listen to texts she doesn't always feel like hearing and to read fragments of a story that never takes shape, something that Garita, between shots of whisky and puffs of marijuana, points out to her. He points it out to her right now:

"All right, all right," – as the delicious fragrance of something with apples and spices baking in the oven wafts through the kitchen – "for eight months I've been listening to your prettied-up version of the little Pasionaria. I already know how her braids bounced up and down, how ardently she spoke to the young recruits, how nicely she sang and danced, but you still haven't told us, among other things, how you're going to begin, that is, if you ever plan to."

"I have several openings," Diana replies dryly.

"Yes, darling," Garita says. "That's your problem. The opening. It doesn't let the bird inside you fly out. What if it turns out to be a parrot that chatters the opening away? No more lectures from me; I'm not about to get into ideologies, because ideologies can build a cathedral from the debris of reality. I'm talking specifically about your sweet little Stalinist soul, and don't get all huffy, just realize that that it leaks out from time to time. And does it ever! All I'm saying is this: you ought to open *yourself* up so you can simply and creatively find a respectable opening for your story. That is, if you have a story at all."

And Diana replies:

"I don't like having my words played with. Open up, huh? Come off it, Kierkegaard, that sounds like a pretty cheap pun for such a clever person. I know quite well what I'm talking about. When I say I have several openings, that's exactly what I mean. Although, to be precise, I only have two, and I've eliminated one of them because it doesn't work, but maybe if I told it to you,

you'd drag out that stupid bird of yours. But I know the real opening is the other one."

And maybe because it's cold and rainy outside (coincidentally, it happens to be the month of July) and because such an appetizing fragrance drifts out from the kitchen that it seems a pity to let bickering ruin this small opportunity for a delightful sanctuary, or because the Bechofen woman, smiling broadly, has just appeared at the kitchen door, or simply because of pride, Diana refrains from telling Garita what she thinks of him and his words, and for the first time, she talks about that freezing July afternoon in 1971 when death stopped being a remote eventuality and she waited for her friend for half an hour at the entrance of the school.

◆

I was captured three months ago, the Thrush tells her. Just when I started to write the report, the prisoner thinks, and yet they kept it from me; even as recently as yesterday they kept it from me, and she feels momentarily annoyed or a little offended. But the Thrush mentions nothing more than generalities about what's happened to him during these three months, and the prisoner is secretly grateful: it excuses her from being too specific herself. It's not easy to relate details about the small acts committed here, not easy to describe those details and for them to be understood. There's an intimacy of acts, a complex network of motives that, judged through a conventional lens, might seem unacceptable, but which, when seen by an unbiased mind, are perfectly comprehensible. The Thrush is intelligent: that much is clear to the prisoner, but she still doesn't know his mindset; she doesn't know what mindset he's adopted under these new circumstances.

But they do perceptively exchange their impressions of the people in this environment, the environment that is now of the greatest interest to them. The prisoner, for example, talks to him at length about the Shark, whom the Thrush hardly knows: a man with a sense of duty but capable of feeling emotion, she says; she omits (she considers it too trivial to mention) the chats in her cubicle, the excursion to the country house, and the evening walks during which physical contact seems imminent but hasn't yet occurred. She also tells him about the psychology of the guards, whom, as they both note, the prisoner has observed more carefully than the Thrush. "It's a question of character," she comments casually, surprising the Thrush with the kindness and cooperative spirit of many of those men the prisoner identifies. The opinions they exchange about people they both know equally well are especially enlightening. Concerning the Falcon, they both agree that he's intelligent and that his recognition of the same quality in them is what made him give preference to them. They don't use the word "preference," but nevertheless it floats between them disturbingly. The Rear Admiral known as Six-fingers, on the other hand, doesn't rate very highly with them: he's brutal and only admits into his circle those who are totally on his side. His lover is a former Montonera nicknamed "Beanie"; she struts around, the prisoner comments, as if she were Mrs. Rear Admiral or something like that. Watch out for that one: she's more dangerous than the soldiers. The Thrush has seen the Admiral only once, yesterday. The prisoner still hasn't met him, but she knows, through the Falcon, that he holds a high opinion of her and wants to meet her soon. Both of them have some notion of their political project, although the Thrush, thanks to that personal conversation, possesses some additional, specific information that might prove very interesting. Both of them have met the Doctor, although they don't specify under what circumstances. In this regard, they recognize a certain, tacit pact of silence, perhaps because under present conditions they don't know what emotional reaction it would provoke; they simply acknowledge that he's a competent professional who's just doing his duty. By way of illustration, the prisoner explains how the

Doctor is going to attend the labour of little Malisa, a young former Montonera whom she's taken under her wing. She doesn't tell him (doesn't think it's necessary) that Malisa is the same woman who came to talk to her when she was being tortured on the table. "They promised me they'll turn the baby over to her parents," the prisoner says proudly. She doesn't dwell on the fact that that promise implies other fates for other newborns, and the Thrush doesn't acknowledge this, either. What he does say is: "I've heard about that girl. Isn't she the one who pretends to be the Angel's sister in some of the training exercises?" They've both seen the Angel: he's blond and impenetrable, but the interesting part, the Thrush tells her, isn't anything he found out from him, but rather from the Falcon. It seems that the Angel, in the heat of an operation, killed a young Swedish girl. "Yes, I knew that," the prisoner says tersely. What you might not know, the Thrush explains, is that the Swedish government has issued a protest and there's growing international disapproval. "You're going to find out that several of our people are in Europe," the Thrush says, giving her a special look, "but there are also some ordinary combatants, all of them doing their part in the campaign to erode the military's prestige." He pauses: the prisoner looks at him expectantly; he foresees a plan, a network of as-yet-invisible projects, like capillaries, but which are there, nonetheless, offering her another chance to make sense of her life. At the same time she experiences a sort of discomfort; in any case, it's the Thrush who's found the thread that will unravel the skein; he's the one who has mentioned the incident of the Swedish teenager and the Angel, he's the one who has seen the Admiral. *This is handled at the level of the Secretaries General* comes back to her from a time that seems distant but which has lodged within her like a recaptured perfume.

"What's the long-range plan?" she asks. The tone is familiar. Anyone who had ever heard her analyzing an operation, presiding over a meeting at the Student Centre, conspiring with other adolescents in white smocks beneath a wisteria arbour, would recognize it. It's a forceful, commanding tone: hearing herself talk is good for her.

The Thrush offers a succinct explanation. Following this explanation, everything follows a normal path. Two heads together, exchanging impressions; the prisoner's firm hand holding a marker and sketching something that wasn't on the paper but which is being born from the heat of their mutual intelligence; calm, yet passionate, voices dreaming up each detail; the prisoner's voice, now enthusiastic, suggesting a name – auspicious, hopeful – for the project; everything that's happening around the table of this little room tastes like the salt of rebirth. If not for the footsteps of the guard, apparently walking back and forth in the confined space outside the door, if not for their ill-concealed startled reaction when they hear someone decisively approaching that door, if not for the prepossessing, authoritarian way in which that door is flung open, an objective observer might observe that the Thrush and the prisoner are still the people they once were.

"How's that project coming along, my esteemed young friends?" the Falcon asks.

Affably, although with a certain guarded irony, the both reply with a smile.

◆

The story will begin, she says, one freezing July afternoon in 1971, a year when death stopped being a remote possibility, although we didn't even suspect (she's thinking) that it would come to this, the siren making us tremble at this very moment in spite of the heady fragrance filtering through the kitchen door, or my fear on a sultry February afternoon at siesta time as I walk down Azopardo, not a soul in the street, and heat that filters down through my body like boiling oil, not a soul except for a soldier in the doorway of a marble building, pointing his rifle: Why? I thought, as I passed in front of the soldier, feeling his gaze on my body and then behind my body because I had passed the marble doorway and I was imagining those eyes following me and I wondered, drenched in terror, what could a soldier with a machine gun be doing out in this beastly sun, what's the only thing he can do to free himself of this silence, this motionlessness, this absurd gesture of meaninglessly aiming into the void, not even daring to pick up my pace to avoid any disturbance that might awaken the soldier or jolt him from his trance into quick, instant action, boom, dead in a confrontation, what history book will give an account of this minor terror I didn't even imagine on that cold afternoon in 1971, although something was beginning to develop, she says, that's why the girl waits so anxiously watching the corner of Cangallo and Díaz Vélez in order not to miss the joy of seeing her approach. Or was it relief? she thinks, wondering if she isn't distorting things a little, if from the very beginning – for some reason she's never made an effort to analyze this – she mightn't have been distorting things a little, and then she would have been betraying her own purpose from the start. And you people may wonder, she says, why the story has to begin there, when almost everything is over, but I believe that's the point, the moment when the girl who's waiting becomes aware of the real risk run by the one she's waiting for. From that point on, the story will advance (where to? she thinks, frightened) and recede until it encompasses the entire life of the one being awaited. Or, to be more precise, whatever the girl who's waiting happens to know about that life.

I'll show, she says, how the waiting girl keeps looking at her watch. Almost half an hour has gone by already, and she's frightened but she knows she won't leave even if she has to remain at that school door till the end of her days (here's where I'll analyze the nature of loyalty and also – maybe later on – how loyalty is learned). Until at last, glancing towards Díaz Vélez, she sees her. Or even more than seeing her – you'll soon find out why – she recognizes her: by her walk and by the way she waves hello with her arm in the air. Suddenly it's as if time hasn't passed, as if, in a certain protected zone, the two of them are still the same people they were. And so the waiting girl, her fear forgotten, raises her arm, too. And a wave of terror floors her. Because as the other woman approaches, what was familiar becomes stranger and stranger. But in order to understand this (she says, looking at the Bechofen woman and at Garita and at the entire, small audience that's gathered in a snug, fragrant place on this night of her departure, while outside it's cold and raining), in order to comprehend the phenomenon that the waiting girl has confirmed, you have to really understand what it's like to be nearsighted. And she pauses to drink the warm, sugary wine that the Bechofen woman has just ladled out for her.

◆

"We've taken an initiative."

The prisoner has just said this, three-and-a-half months before her departure, when neither she nor the other four people around the table suspect anything about a secret escape on a cold, rainy night.

"Speak," commands Sixfingers.

"We've planned the formation of a work unit," the prisoner says.

Seated around the table, Sixfingers, the Falcon, the Shark, and the Angel don't bother to conceal a gesture of dubiousness. It seems like a joke: *they're* the ones who form work units for their operations.

"What do you people think you're whipping up, señora?" Sixfingers says scornfully.

But Sixfingers isn't the one who counts here, the prisoner thinks, and neither are the other three. The one who counts is the Admiral, and his presence weighs on this room like a law. He's the one that the four people sitting around the table are thinking about, and it's before him that the prisoner flaunts her regained security.

"Let me finish, Rear Admiral, sir," she says. "The novelty of the project is, above all, the name it's going to have." She gazes at them, one by one. "I'm proposing to call it the Recovery Group."

Sixfingers looks at her suspiciously.

"Why Recovery?" he asks.

"Because we're going to recover them from death," she had told the Thrush. "Just a few of them, you're right about that, but it's all the same: I see it as a kind of resurrection."

"Some of them can be rehabilitated," she says. "You all know that better than anyone. People who are able to see their own mistakes and understand the reason for what you're doing. But it wouldn't be easy for them to collaborate with you. As you know, 'collaboration' is a dirty word."

"For you," Sixfingers says ferociously.

"It's precisely about *us*, Rear Admiral, sir, if I haven't misunderstood the Admiral's objectives. About how to win the confidence of some of us. I believe we're better equipped to achieve it than you are. There are some very well-qualified people here, and I believe those people are of interest to the Admiral." She looks at the Falcon, who's smiling slightly. "I understand that on the outside, a negative image of the Argentine government is growing. We can help you turn it around. But in order to do that, you need a team of qualified people. That's what I was driving at. Let's say you need an Italian translator and it turns out there's an excellent one here. You bring him to us and we'll be in charge of 'recovering' him. And that's how we'll form the team you'll need."

"Need for what?" Sixfingers asks.

"Let's not waste time, Rear Admiral," the Falcon says. "The lady knows exactly why she's been called in here. It's no secret that we need to reverse the image those sons of bitches are spreading inside and especially outside of the country. Qualified people like them are the ones who can help us with the methods and language we need to use. Right now, as if we didn't have enough problems, the mothers of those criminals are getting together; and you know that the word 'mother' is dangerously powerful. We need to find out what they're plotting, infiltrate their ranks and pretend to be on their side, but in order to do that, we have to know how they speak, what sorts of things convince them. In short: the Admiral wants to know about the movement from within. Who better than they?"

"That's just it," the prisoner says. "We can provide you with methods and select the people." She pauses. "And train them. So, then, what do you think of the name, Rear Admiral, sir?"

"Words, words," Sixfingers says. "Words are useless."

"They have an undeniable psychological effect," the Falcon says. "Let's not forget what element we're dealing with."

"That's exactly what I was referring to," the prisoner says.

"Fuck psychology," Sixfingers says. "I want results."

◆

The result produced is a pause. A not-insignificant pause because she takes advantage of it to drink warm wine with sugar, cinnamon, and a vague hint of lemon, while outside it keeps raining. And since that wine produces a state of confusion in which they can all momentarily forget about themselves and death (sanctuary, my child – the Bechofen woman will tell her, but much later, when it will all somehow be too late – we all need sanctuary sometimes, a lap where we can rest from the horrors of the world, and looking at it from a distance, isn't it true that those meetings of ours weren't so bad, despite the rain and despite death lying in wait for us outside, while we passionately discussed our words and ideas, and festively shared a goulash, a bean stew, a hearty peasant dish, little embers of happiness that made us remember – and why not, when you said so yourself one night, although in different words? – made us remember that life is, has the obligation to be, something beautiful and joyful that's still worth fighting for), and all of them, even Garita, drink and temporarily celebrate life; the Bechofen woman takes advantage of the moment to bring in a delicious *Apfelstrudel* ("Tonight my heart told me it was a night for eating something sweet," she explained); and the Chilean woman whose husband died in the stadium says, "You, Hertha, are arbitrary" – sensually sniffing the strudel – "and timely: you don't turn up your nose at anything." "Ah, my child," the Bechofen woman tells her, "every well-prepared dish has years of wisdom behind it. And a story. A story of deprivation or wealth or slavery or celebration. Every dish of food worthy of the name is an act of love and a synthesis, from porridge to ragout. You just have to know how to prepare it and when to serve it; in that way it's like literature"), an *Apfelstrudel* that everyone celebrates with applause and dives into without hesitation, washed down with warm wine. For which reason Diana's story will be interrupted until the moment when the stutterer asks:

"And what's it like to be nearsighted?"

But by then circumstances will be different from when the tale began.

◆

On a pleasant May morning two months before her departure, two happy events take place. One is a labour and delivery starring little Malisa. The prisoner is at her side, stroking her forehead, and the Shark is there, too: nothing in this world (he says) could have made him miss this childbirth. The entire scene is very moving, except for a brief disturbance that takes place half an hour before a new human being's head peeks out into the world. Someone had spread little Malisa's legs apart at the exact moment when the Shark and the Doctor entered the infirmary. "No, no, you bastards!" little Malisa had shouted, with a spark of terror in her eyes that made the prisoner turn her head away. Then she saw something that frightened her: the Shark's expression. A few seconds later it had passed. All that was left was little Malisa's

148

panting, her efforts to bring a child into the world. Now the tiny head peeks out, and all is hope in the infirmary. The prisoner feels moved: in this same basement where the screams and groans of pain of women in childbirth have been heard and will continue to be heard, unlucky women who will never get to see the children they delivered, in this same basement the miracle of life is about to be produced. And so they don't have to plan it. At the very moment when a newborn boy's cries erupt in the infirmary, the second happy event takes place. Maybe it's the Shark whose hand first seeks the prisoner's; maybe it's the prisoner's hand that takes the initiative. It doesn't matter much. For the prisoner's private story this will always be the first contact: two hands seeking, and finding, one another, while in the basement of the School a baby cries.

◆

"A nearsighted person," Diana says on the rainy night of her departure, unusually expansive from the sugary wine and the prevailing ambiance of good cheer, "as you all know, can't distinguish distant objects; therefore, beyond a certain limit (which varies according to the viewer), she has to imagine reality. Or to be more precise, beyond a few elements of undeniable certainty (a colour, the rhythm of a movement, or something truly huge), she has to do her best to create a whole; something like what Lévi-Strauss does with native communities. And that's what happens to the girl who waits. When she spots her friend coming down Díaz Vélez, the one approaching is so far away that the girl who's waiting never could have recognized her. But a certain way of waving her arm, a rhythm to the approaching woman's walk, makes her say: that's her. It's more than an affirmation; it's a rebirth: not only is the approaching woman not dead, but her familiar greeting evokes for both of them a time that was beautiful. It's important to understand this in order to appreciate the horror that will soon become apparent, as the approaching woman draws nearer. Because just then, the girl who waits will begin to distinguish certain highly visible traits (her hair, her clothing, something about her mouth) and will realize, horrified, that she's made a mistake. The woman approaching is somebody else. That's the problem: in order to understand the exact nature of that horror, you have to assume the subjectivity of the near-sighted observer. But it doesn't make sense, you see. That's not at all what I want to describe."

She sees the Bechofen woman slightly arching her brows. She's about to explain something to her, when Garita says:

"I note another problem. One has every right to ask why the girl isn't wearing glasses."

Then Diana, perhaps a bit tipsy from the warm wine, or from the second helping of *Apfelstrudel*, or from a new aroma, this time reminiscent of her childhood, coming from the kitchen – the Bechofen woman has left the room, no doubt to check on something else in the oven, but she hasn't closed the door – explains, excitedly, that therein lies the secret, the rosebud, the myopic's kernel of truth. Wearing glasses, she says, is like substituting a postcard for a Cézanne landscape, since a myopic person's view (something others don't understand) is much more beautiful than a normal human being's, without even taking into account the fact that anything worth seeing eventually winds up drawing closer to you, or you to it, she says, and none of her listeners can imagine how lovely the night sky looks; I swear (she says), the first time I stepped out on the balcony at night with glasses on I nearly cried. The real moon is nothing compared to that enormous halo I see. Seriously, the fuzziness allows you to imagine whatever you like. Reality and fantasy then become totally useless concepts because all borders are erased. Shapes become versatile and dynamic. As if the world had been designed by some over-the-top impressionist.

She seems so enthusiastic that everyone, including Garita, regards her as though seeing her for the first time, and the

Bechofen woman, who has opened the oven to check on the *Mandelbrot*, foresees something larger than life, some event that is developing too soon. "It's dangerous," she thinks, "for something that's been contained to burst out uncontrollably, against one's will," and she shakes her head dubiously because this, she says to herself, needs more time in the oven.

◆

"The Shark said you wanted to see me," says Hernández the Chimp, the man who once played the guitar like a dream. He says this one month before her departure.

He's standing in the prisoner's cubicle, looking all around with a mixture of incredulity and displeasure.

"I wanted to make a few observations, yes," the prisoner says.

"Regarding what?" the Chimp says, aggressively.

"Books, the classification of the books. The Thrush and I think you're not following the classification criteria we created."

"And?"

"And that throws an entire system of analysis into disorder. The Thrush and I spent a lot of time thinking up those criteria; it wasn't so easy with all the material we had to work with; we went over it again and again, trying to figure out how to classify all those books, so that some valid conclusions might be reached."

"For whose benefit?" the Chimp says, in a very quiet voice.

"That's another issue entirely. If I do something, no matter what it is, I can't do it halfway. Either I do it perfectly or I don't do it. And the Thrush is exactly the same way."

"Fuck your sense of perfection and fuck his, too. Me, I'm just doing my damndest to keep them from killing me." He lowers his voice even more. "But I have no interest in making things easy for those bastards."

"Whether you like it or not, you *are* making it easier for them." The prisoner is now speaking very quietly as well, so that they must stand very close to one another in order to hear one another. "And, besides, the Thrush and I are in charge of this plan. So we get to dictate the terms."

"Very noble of you and the Thrush. And how does he feel about this nice little love nest of yours?"

"I don't know what you mean."

"I mean I get nauseous looking at these little flowers you stuck on the walls to cover up the spectacle of death."

"Would fewer people die if I lived in a pigsty? They wouldn't, would they? Well, then, I prefer to look at pretty things."

"Yeah, right, ask them to take you to visit the place where the future dead are crammed together, that place you were kind enough to rescue three or four people from. I was there, and I guarantee you'll see pretty things. And smell pretty things, too. It smells of shit, and fear. You know what fear smells like?"

"No."

"You're lying. I smelled fear on you when you were chained naked to a cot, with your arms and legs spread. Or don't you remember the day they brought me in to soften you up?"

"Yes, I remember. You came and tempted me. You weren't the only one, but let's say you were the one who gave me confidence; you were one of mine. And, I don't know, now I wonder why you were there, what you did to get out of being crammed in there with the others."

"The same thing all of us do who get out and live to tell about it. But, I, at least, hate them. And sometimes I hate myself."

"What a great feat. Your guts get knotted up every time you work for them, and that must make you feel like a hero."

"I don't feel like a hero; I feel like a rat."

"But you work for them, regardless. I, on the other hand, don't work for them."

"You're a leader."

"I try to exercise my authority. And I really believe in what I'm doing. I tell myself: it has to be like this and like that, and I try to do it in the best possible way. That makes me feel at peace with myself."

"You're what's known as a happy person."

"I'm happy, yes. I'm alive. And I've got my daughter back."

"At what price?"

"At the price a daughter is worth. How do you like that?"

"I love it. And to top it all off, you have a fancy little love nest, and you go for secret walks in the afternoon, and you help some kid who goes out in the street identifying people, pregnant and all, and who's slept with every official who's ever asked her for it, you help her give birth. And meanwhile they steal other pregnant women's babies, and then they throw the mothers in the river with all the other miserable wretches who don't have your sense of perfection."

"I'm not the one who kills them. I save as many as I can. If I were dead, would that be possible?"

"You're helping those criminals; you're killing those people yourself."

"They're not criminals; that's the point. They believe what they're doing is the best way to eliminate subversion."

"Just like you. They believe in what they're doing; now I get it. And by the way, you didn't answer my question. Does the Thrush know you have this fancy little room?"

"That's my business," the prisoner replies brusquely. "No one has the right to stick his nose in my business. And if you understand what I mean about the books, there's nothing else for us to talk about."

◆

They talk, they talk incessantly, as if the warm wine and Diana Glass's enthusiasm and the rain falling outside, in a space that

153

can't touch them, had opened the lid of a festive box and everyone had just discovered some hidden anecdote about their good or bad vision. The stutterer talks about a fishing gear salesman who boarded the bus a few days ago. "Practically blind. Only sees shapes," the stutterer reports, beautifully condensed, what the fishing gear salesman had said about his condition, and the Chilean woman whose husband died in the stadium talks about the time they put drops in her eyes to dilate her pupils, and when she went out into the street (it was already dark), she nearly lost her mind: the lights were gigantic circles impinging on other circles, the approaching car headlights threatened to devour her, the traffic lights covered the treetops, reality had become a psychedelic paradise.

There is a silence, and in the middle of that silence, Garita's voice can be heard, surprised, like someone who's just discovered something extraordinary.

"Look," he says thoughtfully, "couldn't it be that Van Gogh was nearsighted, after all? His hallucinatory stars, couldn't they be stars seen by myopic eyes?"

Behind his words, and behind the rain, so distant it seems unreal, they hear gunfire.

Diana grows alert.

"In any event," she says (now silence has returned behind the rain), "I don't really care if Van Gogh was nearsighted or farsighted. I didn't come to this house to sample cookies and digress about vision problems. I came here because I wanted to find the way to tell a very specific story."

(And the worst part is that it wasn't true. The worst part is that I desperately needed to talk about my myopia, and about the colossal moon of my childhood, and about the strange shapes I sometimes perceive where others see only a raincoat on a hanger. In spite of the horror, in spite of the fear, in spite of death. And perhaps at the very moment I became furious with Garita, I was already beginning to foresee what later – too late? – I would discover completely. That the

proximity of death doesn't cure you of madness; it doesn't even cure you of joy. And so, if I left them out, if I pushed away the touch of recklessness that seized me as I sensibly tried to make the others understand how Leonora's image appeared and disappeared on that July afternoon in 1971, if my embarrassment made me suppress the fleeting giddiness that made us laugh despite the fact that death still lurked outside the door of my house and outside every door, if I left out the chaos, I would never manage to really describe the horror. My horror. Because my horror was that I was alive, cruelly, ferociously assailed by the unbearable desire to live and laugh and be happy. And the intolerable guilt of being alive. That was the horror I had to tell: joy, and fear, and guilt, and rage, and impotence, and disgust, all coexisting inside me during that merciless winter of 1977.

"What I'm beginning to realize," she says, "is that I'll never find what I'm looking for in this nuthouse. And forgive me, Garita, for what I'm about to say, but I haven't been coming here all these months just to listen to you. I came because I admired that woman," pointing spitefully towards the kitchen door. "I thought she could help me. But I was wrong. She's capricious and vain; she sticks her head through that door like a star and says 'pickled herring' or 'stuffed cunt,' then off she goes, pleased as punch, to prepare her concoctions just as though she were living in the kingdom of the Marquis of Carrabas."

"Nice allusion to *Puss in Boots*," Garita says.

"Shut up for once in your life. Don't you see how ridiculous you are, always looking behind my words for God-knows-what *you* want to see, but it has nothing to do with what I meant. No. This isn't what I came for, to take lessons from a reactionary faggot loser."

"You've got to admit I never misled you," says Garita, unruffled.

"I've got to admit that, right. Ever since that first night in the kitchen, you showed your true colours, so I shouldn't have been

155

surprised when I heard you talk about 'my little Pasionaria' a while ago without blinking an eye at the thought that the Pasionaria you're talking about is dead, like so many others, while we spout off about myopia just because our heads are full of wine or because we're afraid to think seriously about what's happening to us. And since you find my literary allusions so interesting, do you know what all this reminds me of? It reminds me of the March Hare's famous tea party. You're the Mad Hatter, and she's the Queen of Hearts, waiting, I don't know what for, the famous moment when the whole deck of cards goes flying through the air. As for me, I won't keep her waiting anymore. Sorry to ruin this charming little party of yours, but I can't take one more minute in this house. I'm leaving."

And without missing a beat, she stood up and put on her coat, just as Hertha Bechofen appeared, outlined against the open kitchen door, with a heaping tray of *Mandelbrot.*

◆

The baptism takes place twenty days before her departure, a simple but moving ceremony, the prisoner's mother thinks. The military priest has found a way to touch her heart: at the moment when he mentions those souls who are lost forever, comparing them with those other wayward souls who, through confession, penance, and repentance, can return to the righteous path, he looks eloquently at her daughter, and her daughter smiles. At the moment, the prisoner's mother feels like she can touch heaven with her hands.

There aren't many in attendance. The priest, the two children about to be baptized, their respective mothers, the Shark and the Angel serving as godparents of the little boy – who will be named Pedro in honour of the Shark, the prisoner whispers in her mother's ear – since he was kind enough to be present at the child's birth, with the prisoner's parents acting as godparents of the girl, Violeta, who, at age ten and at her mother's decision

156

(her father wasn't consulted because he's dead), will at last receive the Holy Oils.

After the ceremony there's a small celebration. They serve delicious hot chocolate accompanied by a variety of finger sandwiches and exchange good wishes for the physical and spiritual health of the children. Everyone chats animatedly and optimistically. The prisoner's mother has another reason to feel happy. Her daughter, who looks so elegant today in her lady-like dress, has been given a very important mission. She still can't provide them with any more details because it's top secret. But within twenty days they'll find out this mission's most attractive aspect.

◆

The Bechofen woman, like a tiny queen bearing her tray of *Mandelbrot*, walked into the room. Which made Diana, with her coat already on, interrupt her sudden movement towards the door, as though she still secretly expected something of that small, wrinkled woman. She deposited the tray on the coffee table and sat on a miniature chair (which forced Diana to sit on the floor in order not to have to look down on her from above, and to reflect later on the difference between someone who has authority and someone who's authoritarian, *someone who plants himself on a platform*, she wrote, *so that you have no other choice but to regard him from below*), speaking to her so sweetly that Diana felt protected by her words, while at the same time knew she had been abandoned by them and could no longer take comfort in them.

"I see you've put on your coat, my dear," she said, "and I'm going to do you the courtesy of not asking you to take it off again. Since you made a decision, the best thing you can do for yourself is not turn back. But I do advise you not to harbour too many illusions about what this means. It doesn't really mean anything at all. No one can turn back. If you were to take off your coat now and decide to stay with us to enjoy this crispy *Mandelbrot* and return every Friday, you'd still be moving forward, but in a state of regret. And that's not a good state to be in. It's more satisfying to confront your outbursts with your own eyes and act accordingly. But before you go, child, hear me out:"

And with a tranquillity Diana learned to appreciate on that very evening, it occurred to her that all her lessons came to her ill timed: *It's not that you're a poor thinker, my dear; it's that you work up the courage to confront your thoughts just when they're losing their potency; that's why you're always stuck in the middle of the road,* the Bechofen woman would tell her much later. From her miniature chair, she spoke to her at length about things that Diana had been too confused to realize.

"Think about it, child," she said by way of conclusion, "most of all, think about it if someday you want to write that novel that seems so hard for you, and remember that unhappiness offers no excuses. We who are alive never have excuses. It's a bad thing when you don't know where to begin, and worse yet when you want to leave madness out of the picture. There's plenty of madness in these times we live in, child, and so, after this time of death, a time of great confusion awaits us."

Then she kissed her on both cheeks, French style, and let her go out into the intemperate night at the very moment when the prisoner, unperturbed by the torrential rain and waving her arm in the air, said goodbye to the Shark (who waved to her from below) from the stairs of the plane in which, a few minutes later, she would leave on a special, secret mission to Paris.

Thirteen

At the Argentine Embassy they thought we were sociologists, she says, sociologists working in co-operation with the government. That is, she and Beanie, she clarifies, because the Jackal was what he was: an ensign working for the Admiral. The Shark wasn't there that time – she referred to him as Pedro – but he came on the third trip, although naturally he did get away, just like the Angel and others; the Admiral himself came every so often because Paris was an important centre for the image change.

But on that first trip, she says, there were three of them in the core group: she, the Jackal, and Beanie, and they lived in a very elegant residential hotel near the Eiffel Tower. She looks out the window with a distant expression; I look out, too: I manage to see the awning of Café Mecca. Living together wasn't as unbearable as I thought it would be, she says, because the Jackal was very involved in picking up women and Beanie in ordering outfits from the big *couture* houses. She herself had had to buy very exclusive clothing, at Christian Dior and Pierre Cardin and other places like that, even though she never liked ostentation – and she points to her body, more voluminous than in her adolescent photos – because those were the Admiral's orders. You mustn't forget that they moved in the very highest circles; what would have happened if they found out she and Beanie had been Montoneras? A major scandal, and with them being there in Paris explicitly to neutralize scandals. You have to understand, she says, that the Mothers of the Plaza de Mayo already existed and the international human rights organizations referred to the Junta as though they were talking about the Third Reich, or worse. Our job was to change that image, she says, so it was essential that they not recognize us. Even at the Embassy, she explains, where not only were there government flunkies, but also career diplomats, and they weren't too crazy about those reports of bodies floating in the river; some of them suspected it was true. She specifically names one woman at the Embassy who was beginning to spread certain dangerous rumours. The Jackal had his eye on her, and between you and me, Leonora confides, he was the one who gave the final order to have the woman killed, but that happened later, when she had already returned from Europe.

No, the idea of escaping never crossed her mind. Escaping what? she asks me, shrugging her shoulders. She says they knew that she wasn't the kind to show up at the United Nations and file a lawsuit. It's not that I approve of torture or throwing people into the sea, she says, but sometimes you have to put sentimentality aside and analyze facts with a clear head. Even with legal trials, they wouldn't have been able to prove very much because the guerrillas acted clandestinely and didn't leave personal evidence behind, and they couldn't hold prisoners indefinitely. Yes, it was true they killed innocent people, but what other possibility was there when there were no trials? Sometimes you have to put yourself in someone else's shoes, she says, and no one has the absolute truth, only God. She casts a quick glance at the ceiling.

Anyway, during that first trip she didn't enjoy Paris much. She didn't go to the museums because they made her feel claustrophobic and she thought she might be recognized there. She had dyed her hair and she went around in high heels and those elegant fashions, but even so: Montoneros had plenty of experience in those things, in changing their appearance. That's why she preferred the parks and boulevards.

As for the tasks themselves, she's less precise; she tucks in the baby, who seems about to wake up, looks out the window again, says they sent newspaper clippings about the Europeans' opinions of Argentina, and they advised the people in Buenos Aires on how to act. Especially me, she says, thumping her chest with a certain show of pride, because the only thing the Jackal wanted was to shoot at the Mothers and the people in the Organizations, and all Beanie wanted to do was get rid of me. It was all about jealousy, she says, since she was in Paris only because she was Sixfingers's lover, while I, on the other hand . . . She smiles at the man who has just entered the room: he's tall and dark and looks like a good person. She tells him the baby isn't up yet, even though it's almost feeding time, and that she needs to continue talking to me, if he doesn't mind. In fact, she tells me after the man leaves the room with the sleeping child, when they returned from the first trip, Beanie told the Admiral that Leonora didn't have to go back to Paris because she seemed to be on good terms with the Social Democrats. She laughs: when you have a humanist's soul, it always slips out somehow, she says. But the Admiral replied that he didn't need a mirror to see himself in: what he wanted to know was what the enemies were thinking – don't forget his project was populist – and the only one equipped to interpret their thoughts was Leonora. And so Beanie shot herself in the foot, she says, laughing, because she didn't get to go on the second trip. Little Malisa replaced her, but that wasn't the best part; the best part was that they let her bring Violeta. This time they rented a three-bedroom apartment on the Rue de Rivoli: the Jackal slept in one bedroom, little Malisa in the other, and she and Violeta occupied the biggest one. But that wasn't the only nice thing about that second stage, she says. On one of the Shark's quick trips – she continues to refer to him as Pedro – by order of the Admiral, both of them were to go on a special mission to London, even more beautiful than Paris, in her opinion; maybe, she says, because my dad always talked about London. And, on a day off, one after-noon as they wandered through Hampstead Heath, the Shark stopped her, looked into her eyes, and said: "It's been exactly one year today." She says she understood later that he was refer-ring to the day they met. She remembered that scene perfectly but until that moment she didn't know the date; she knew it was in October because she was captured in October, but those first few weeks in the basement, she couldn't tell if it was day or night, so of course she didn't remember the dates. His words surprised her, she says: that he was attracted to her from that very first time. She doesn't believe it entirely, not because she thinks the Shark is a liar – Pedro doesn't lie, she says – but because she thinks he's deceiving himself. I was covered with piss and shit, she says; I imagine my mouth was all swollen from the *picana*, and my eyes, too. And the Shark isn't the sort to get turned on by a woman on the torture table, as he himself has told her: others do, but not him; others poke the cattle prod in, and if they don't rape the victim, they don't get off. But when-ever he stuck the *picana* in a vagina, he was simply applying a technique. Like doing pushups. That's how we soldiers are, she says he told her one day. Crossing the Andes or twisting balls. If it's your duty, you do it. That's why, she says, she doesn't believe he was attracted to her at first sight. But that afternoon, in Hampstead Heath, after he reminded her of their first anniver-sary, they looked at each other for a few moments, and at last they kissed. And it was beautiful, after such a difficult year, to kiss in that splendid park. And that night, for the first time, they made love.

On the third trip (shortly after this episode the group had returned to Buenos Aires to report in), the Jackal was eliminated for inefficiency and they sent the Shark in his place. Those were the best days, she says, because on top of all the other blessings, after a short time, little Malisa went to live with some guy named Renato, who had also been a Montonero and now was co-operating openly with the military. And I mean openly. On the other side. But not her; she was simply performing a job they had assigned her. And she tried to do the best possible job. Just like the Thrush, she says, who won't even say hello to me now. And some others. Just like when she was a physicist: she might have been doing research that would be useful to capitalism, but that didn't stop her from fighting for the revolution. And like right now, over there – pointing upward, supposedly towards the place in South America where she lives – she designs projects for multinationals, but that doesn't prevent her from being interested and participating in national political projects of broad scope. And love is something else. When little Malisa left, the three of them were alone in the apartment – she, Violeta, and the Shark, whom she keeps calling Pedro – and they were a family. She and the Shark slept in the master bedroom, and Violeta was delighted because she had a room to herself. An ideal situation. Of course Violeta loved the Shark. And she still loves him, she says firmly. You mustn't forget he was the one who saved her life. No, in fact he wasn't the one who killed Fernando: in a military operation, everyone is a cog. You have a purpose to fulfill, and that's that. No, Violeta never mentions Fernando; there are many things she doesn't talk about, but getting back to the subject, they were very happy in Paris, the three of them in that apartment on the Rue de Rivoli. A family. And ever since 1971, she hadn't had a family, a house where she could open the windows in the morning and be greeted by the neighbours. *Bonjour, votre fille comment est-elle? Et votre mari?* But, of course, that was the idyllic part of the third trip, because the other part wasn't going well. The group had grown; several of the Admiral's representatives were collaborating with them, but that didn't improve things. The World Cup was coming soon, and it was necessary to

163

do everything they could to combat the negative propaganda. There were even books in circulation with the names of the disappeared and reports about the School and other detention centres, and the Mothers were beginning to travel around the world airing their problems. On top of everything else, one of the Mothers recognized the Angel in Paris. She accused him of the business about the Swedish teenager and of the murder of some French nuns, and so there was an international scandal. Getting him out of France hadn't been easy; if it hadn't been for Pedro and me, she says, he wouldn't be dancing in clubs today. They got him out on a tourist train crossing the Pyrenees. He pretended to be travelling alone; in his brightly coloured shirt, his Bermudas, and sunglasses, he was the perfect Yankee tourist, and she and the Shark were a very proper couple, watching closely. But things were never the same after that. For a while they shifted their activities to Spain, but that was worse; Spain was full of Argentines. All of Europe, in fact, with *Videla is a Murderer* signs and other stuff like that. They were ordered to return, and in Buenos Aires life wasn't so easy. She lived with the Shark and Violeta, yes, and that was lovely, but she went around frightened. She was always afraid someone from the Organization would recognize her. Besides, it was as though she wasn't anywhere at all, or as though she had no mission, which is the same thing: just like floating aimlessly. She advised the Admiral, of course. She told him how to treat the Mothers, what to say to the Grandmothers, concrete things like that. Because you'd be surprised, she says, the military seems very strict, but they're pretty innocent about a lot of things. That is, they're very decisive about war matters, but in other ways . . . Just think of the Admiral, for example: he organizes everything at the School; he trains an elite team of collaborators, and then he doesn't know what to do with it. She told him, "Carrying out a political project, Admiral, isn't like blowing bubbles." You're born with it. She didn't tell him that last part, but it's a fact; you carry activism in your blood. And that's what happened to her: she could no longer give orders or work or anything. It was hard, because she had always been a woman of action. For the first time in her life she felt lost.

◆

Completely ill-timed. Ill-timed in her life and in the history of the nation, a leap of her soul or a burst of unruliness that propels her, as it propelled her beneath the tree during the springtime of the tree, to cross Calle Florida near Corrientes with as much energy and useless elation as though she were a runner who had suddenly glimpsed her goal. It's not a serious inconvenience that on this sunny afternoon in 1979 she isn't fourteen, but rather thirty-six, and that her horizon is totally devoid of goals. Nor does it matter that the traffic light – which she hasn't even seen – is red.

It's then that something piercing and perverse crosses behind her.

It's a whistle, so imperious that it freezes her in her tracks. From the very source of fear, from the back of her head, an unmistakable sign has reached her: that whistle comes from the Powers That Be and is possibly directed at her. Without turning her head, she waits. The whistle blows again. And a woman's voice orders:

"You, in the red sweater! Halt!"

She looks at her chest; of course, it's her. With undignified fear, she turns around. A few feet away, a stubby woman in an impeccable blue hat nails her with a fierce glance.

"Me?"

The woman in the hat doesn't bother to answer. From the edge of the sidewalk she puffs out her cheeks exaggeratedly, and for the third time, blows her whistle.

Toot-toot, don't shoot, thinks Diana. The joke pleases her, despite her rotten luck.

"Honestly, I don't know what I did," she says. Forewarned, she's speaking from six feet away from the woman in the hat, which causes her to raise her voice a little. People watch from a prudent distance, seemingly poised to walk away whistling to themselves the minute the incident stops being amusing.

"You don't know what you did!" The woman in the hat sweeps her glance around at the small audience, fixes it on Diana, plants her hands on her hips, and says, "Hmmm." Diana realizes that she's waiting for a gesture of contrition, but doesn't know what she's supposed to be sorry for.

"I mean," she says, "I don't think I did anything wrong."

"You didn't do anything wrong!" says the woman in the hat, outraged, looking at the audience again. Now she turns to Diana. "You were crossing on a red light!" she shouts at her, as though she were about to pounce.

"I'm sorry," Diana says.

"You're sorry? And if you killed your mother, would you just say you're sorry?" Diana tries to decide if this is a rhetorical question or if the voice of authority doesn't recognize this linguistic device and if all her questions should be answered. But fortunately, the woman in the hat solves the problem for her. "I can see there are many violations you don't know about because now, in addition to committing an infraction, you're being disrespectful."

"Disrespectful?" Diana asks, realizing with alarm that she's adopted the official's repetitive style.

"Affirmative," says the woman in the hat. "You've disobeyed my orders and are in a state of defiance, in the middle of the street."

Diana turns her head, desperately looking for something.

"It's green now," she says, just as the light turns yellow. She carefully approaches the sidewalk.

"Give me your documents," the woman with the hat orders.

Red alert. She's sure that something subversive will emerge from her document, and as soon as the woman in the hat has it in her hands, she'll discover some serious flaw in it, something that won't allow her to walk away.

"Why? Why do you need my document?"

"Because I'm going to write you a ticket," says the woman with the hat.

"A ticket? I don't think I'm a car," she says in her best, jocular, nice-girl tone. She looks at the woman in the hat and understands that she's not the best audience for jokes. She doesn't hear anyone else laughing, either.

"That's the new ordinance," the woman with the hat says, impassively. "Any pedestrian who commits an infraction gets a ticket."

"But I didn't know," Diana says. "Besides, I'm very absent minded."

"If you killed your mother, would you just say you were very absent minded?" asks the woman in the hat.

Diana has no response to this question. "I could run away; after all, they can't take my licence plate number," she thinks, somewhat facetiously. But the woman in the hat opens her purse to remove something, and Diana can see her weapon. Frightened, she hands over her identification paper.

She watches the woman with the hat open it, look at the photo, and look at her with the seriousness of someone who's verified that the person she has before her is, in effect, the same one who appears on the WANTED posters.

Then she takes out a ticket book, and glancing at the document from time to time, begins to write. Diana moves in closer and surreptitiously watches what she's writing:

Name of Driver: Diana Glass

Registration Number: 4-638-272

Licence Plate Number:

It's obvious they don't have the budget to print tickets under this new regime, she thinks, leaning her head a little closer; she's anxious to see how the woman with the hat is going to resolve the licence plate number problem. There it is: she's written it down. **Licence Plate Number:** pedestrian. She worked it out pretty well, she thinks. And it occurs to her that there's something coarse about the word "pedestrian." Or slyly pejorative. Once she saw a photo of a park in Vancouver. *This road is for pedestrians only,* read a sign at the edge of the path. Quite different: Canadian pedestrians have paths for themselves; everyone else keep off, you're not entitled to this privilege. Here on the other hand, a pedestrian not only lacks privileges, he's a sort of invalid: he walks because he has no car, tough shit. And to top it all off, he's a potential delinquent.

Model: woman, age 36.

Chassis number: erased.

No doubt national cleverness compensates for the lack of resources, she thinks.

"What are you looking at?"

Diana raises her head, startled. She takes a step back.

"The thing is, I'm nearsighted," she says, regretting the words as soon as she pronounces them, wondering if they'll increase her fine for going around without eyeglasses.

But no. The penalty will be determined by a Traffic Court, before which the lawbreaker must appear posthaste, and before which she abashedly recognizes she will indeed appear since she has no way of anticipating the consequences of not showing up at that court or any other, although neither can she anticipate the consequences of showing up; for all she knows, she might already have been judged guilty, perhaps at the moment when, seized by a totally ill-timed joy, she crossed the street on a red light. Her fate was already sealed, a fate that, as she stands at the intersection of Corrientes and Florida, she tries fruitlessly to decipher in a crude, little light blue ticket that informs her that her chassis number has been erased, not to mention her turn signal, my God, she has absolutely no turn signal whatsoever; she isn't carrying a fire extinguisher; she's been despoiled of low beams; doesn't display a rear-view mirror; goes around without tail lights. And, to top it all off, she's standing all alone at the intersection of Corrientes and Florida, feeling the hateful gaze of the woman in the hat on the back of her neck, a woman who could easily strike her with her whistle or some other lethal weapon; armed with a little piece of blue paper and a very familiar sensation, she can't stop laughing at how ridiculous and outrageously funny reality can be, even in the midst of fear. It's something (she vaguely begins to understand) that Garita had tried to communicate to her a year and a half ago, and that the Bechofen woman, especially, tried to communicate to her with her stews and her sweets and her terseness, as she pronounced from her miniature chair, my dear, someone has to give an account of this quagmire and say, without solemnity, that horror and fear and prowling death, don't eliminate – not one bit – the desire to laugh. That, too, is evil, being taken unawares in the throes of life, when you thought you still had all your stories left to live, and all your stories left to tell, being attacked from behind and left with just one story, the only one that seems to make sense in times of death. These criminals, my child, who burst into houses and destroy people and people's things, also destroy something in those of us who by chance remain alive. They destroy that delicate, capricious storyline we began weaving in less beastly times and which made us human. I was looking for a story, child; forty years ago I was looking for a story that would have the serene structure of daily life but would at the same time admit, like a subtle glow, the madness and cruelty and magic that secretly inspire human actions. But they demolished all delicate structures. For those of us who weren't blind, the poetic impulse, and the gift of humour, and the desire to change the world, and the love that seasons aromatic dishes as they're prepared in kitchens, and love, ah, love, it all disappeared, brutally replaced by indignation and fear. They broke us, my child, they broke us in the throes of life. And yet, inside each one of us, those of us who are alive and those who are going to die, there burns the desire to live. As full and complex and contradictory as life should be. Let it burn, child, between the cracks of horror and against the dealers of death. And she, at the intersection of Corrientes and Florida, with the blue paper in her hand, laughs outrageously at the woman in the hat and at all the uniformed and plainclothes officials who try to eradicate from human beings all traces of what they might have been, in the name of her dead friend and of all the dead, dreamers of a world of joy they'll never see, she, too, pledges to rescue all the little stories that keep filtering through the cracks of fear, like wounds open to hope, or like a slash against those who mutilate them in the throes of life.

She's in the midst of this resolution or rejoicing when two hands cover her eyes. She touches those hands, soft and seemingly boneless, melting into the contours of her face. She's touching those hands but she doesn't dare speak. I'm insane, she thinks, trying to free herself of what's holding her. Then she hears the voice falling on the back of her head.

"Diana," the voice says.

She pronounces the name and turns around.

She feels like she's dying.

Fourteen

"And then I discovered two things," she says. She pauses.

She's returned after nearly two years; she's been talking for more than half an hour and seems very tired. She looks at the Bechofen woman and all the others as if just now recognizing them. But she's still so lost – or so desperate at what's happened to her and what she's just related at length – that she doesn't even notice that Garita isn't there.

"The first thing I discovered is that I'm never going to be able to write that novel anymore."

"*That* novel, my dear, is something you were never going to be able to write anyway. Because that novel was always just half a story. Now, at least, you're beginning to have a whole story."

"You don't understand me, Hertha. It's not a question of what I have or don't have. It's a question of what I wanted to tell. The story of a woman who, until the last, pursued our dream of a world we wouldn't have to be ashamed of. It was, I don't know, homage to a generation, to the dead of a generation that heard the school bell ring and thought it could touch socialism with its hands. And to the survivors of that generation, too – yes, why not? We had it all, don't you see? A childhood among lazy, pleasant streets, ground that seemed solid, and hope for a better world. Too much to lose as we did. That's why I needed a heroine, to focus her story like a lens. Or like a credo in spite of everything. I nurtured that story for years, please understand what I'm trying to say; I protected it from all harm so that nothing beneath our dream could harm it. And one fine day I came face to face with the protagonist. Can you imagine that scene? Suddenly there I was with her repulsive, unchanging smile, sitting right across from me at a table at the Café Richmond and telling me about some Admiral's popular project and about billing and cooing like a turtledove with a torturer."

"From a literary angle, my dear, the only problem I see is that you still lack the energy to assimilate that stranger."

"Maybe that's not the worst of it, Hertha. Maybe the worst of it is that the woman who spoke to me for two hours at a table at the Richmond should never have been a stranger to me. And that's the second thing I discovered." She extracts her yellow-leafed notebook from a large briefcase. "The second thing I discovered is how to do the first chapter."

Then, for the first time, she looks at the place where Garita should have been and appears about to ask something. But the Bechofen woman stops her with a gesture of her hand.

"Read, my child, we'll talk about that later," she tells her. "We're all anxious to listen to you."

Then Diana takes out her glasses, opens the yellow-leafed notebook, and fleetingly overcome with feeling, in a slightly emotional voice that she tries to control as she continues reading, pronounces the words with which she has at last constructed the episode where the non-activist friend waits for the activist one at the door of a school *that incredibly is on a street whose name means Hope – Calle Esperanza –* (she reads) *although at the time of this meeting, they had already changed its name, and it's not a metaphor for what I'm about to tell. It's strange (if not always encouraging) to discover how life constructs certain ironies.* It's a dusty July afternoon. It's understood that the one who waits is anxious and fears for the life of the one who's about to arrive. Then, perhaps in order to mitigate her uneasiness, she suddenly thinks that she should give an account of that exuberant, and in a way exemplary, life. *She had been born to drink life down to the bottom of the glass*, she thinks, as though she had already written it. But the thought is barely a gust of wind because at that moment, in the distance, she thinks she can see the one who should be arriving. She feels a sense of relief that immediately changes into a foreboding of disaster: the woman approaching isn't the one she was waiting for. At that point the narration is interrupted by some considerations about myopia, and Diana casts a quick, complicit glance at her small audience. But now that the woman is approaching, the opposite phenomenon is confirmed. The stranger with short, dark hair, dressed in a severe business suit, reveals that the unmistakable olive skin and broad smile – now the girl who waits can verify them – are heading purposefully towards her. There's a rushing together and an embrace that recalls another one on a distant, golden afternoon, and a short walk during which the newly arrived woman, notably taller than the one who was waiting, slips her arm around her shoulders. There is – the girl who was waiting thinks – an atmosphere of intimacy that invites recollection of lost time, as if in a certain protected zone they were still two young readers of Salgari who would dream of changing the world. They chat. Or rather, the one who was waiting asks and the newly arrived one answers, quickly, expeditiously, about the twists and turns of political activity, about its effectiveness, about alliances and strategies. (Something, she doesn't know what, is bothering the one who waited: her tone? Her language? And she doesn't want her negative bias to cast a shadow over this special moment.) "But are you all okay?" she asks, cleverly shifting the conversation towards calmer waters. "We are, yes," answers the newly arrived one. "We're . . ." She cuts herself short, abruptly saying: "The little one's with my parents. They need to enroll her in kindergarten. Here." And before the girl who was waiting can react, she thrusts something into her hands, something that at first glance looks like a handful of papers, hugs her fiercely, and takes off. "Take them to my parents' house; try to do it right away," she shouts as she walks away.

Following this is a description of the waiting girl's state of shock, her momentary paralysis, her discovery (which she omits, out of embarrassment for the other woman) of the reason why the newly arrived one fled as soon as she left this in her hands (she looks it over as she stands on the corner by the school): it's exploding gunpowder, the complete documents of the two most wanted people in Buenos Aires, which she now must bring – which she unwaveringly will bring, in the name of Yáñez and the Little Match Girl – to a house that is undoubtedly being watched, carefully calculating that she may well become one more news item among those that are starting to be published these days and that contribute, albeit unknowingly, to the construction of a new and frightening definition of the word "disappeared," even without anyone's having asked her if she accepts this modest role in the struggle. *The end justifies the means*, the girl who waited tells herself flippantly, forbidding herself to be frightened as she advances towards the designated house. The rest is foreseeable: the walk over there, with humiliating stomach cramps; the dissembling wait at the bus stop until a policeman, posted very near the house, turns the corner, momentarily disappearing from view; entering the house in order to carry out her little mission.

"Now do you understand what I mean?" she says. "The story I wanted to tell ends, it always ended, in that first chapter. Because the awaited woman will never fight, never wanted to fight, the same revolution that the one who awaited her hoped for. That's what was happening to me. Garita was right; he always suspected something wasn't working, and he hit the nail on the head. I couldn't go forward; I couldn't see beyond a certain point in that first chapter, simply because if I had seen beyond, the story would have ended for me right then and there," she laughs. "So now I wear glasses." She stops laughing. "Where's Garita?" she asks suddenly, as if something violent had just startled her awake.

"Disappeared," the Bechofen woman says. "No, my child, he was no hero. He didn't run out into the street, shouting '¡Viva la Revolución!' 'Death to the military motherfuckers!' Although he might as well have shouted it, why not, and I want to say in tribute to him that at the end he must have said it, looking his torturers straight in the eye and revealing his contempt with his very last breath. He's dead now, I know that; he wasn't the kind to make a good impression on those bastards. It's a paradox, really, although not a huge one; he might have fit into that story you wanted to tell. That you still want to tell, I hope. I, at least, still wish for a world where Garita might fit in. Annoying, homosexual, abrasive, deliberately enraging those who listened to him, but surely diving headfirst into the jaws of the enemy sooner than leaving you alone with your fear. They must have had their reasons for taking him away. It's not worth telling; he was no hero, but this isn't a story about heroes, my dear; it's a story about murder and murderers. And it's also a story about survivors. Not an easy thing you're living through. *We're* living through. Bah, life is inexhaustible, my child: have you ever heard it said of some venerable old man that he's come back from everything? It's a lie: one can never be back from anything; there's no return trip, my child. Here you have me, the Queen of Hearts, sitting on a little bench. So, forget your heroine and tell what you have to tell."

"It isn't what I wanted."

"History is never what one wants, my dear. But it doesn't matter. If it doesn't feel right for you to write the story, I'll write it myself. For a while now I've been looking for an interesting character; now I have two."

"Go on and try, Hertha, but you won't be able to. Now I know the story well. I know that it will end for you in the first chapter. The character already shows her colours there."

"That's literature, my dear, and yes, if one really makes the effort," she gazes at her intently, "literature ends up more or less resembling what one wants. Besides, don't boast so about knowing your story. You were outraged too soon. We would have to know more about that woman in order to tell it."

"Impossible. As I told you, she left the country. And that might be the only good news lately. I don't want to see her again. She tore my own story to shreds, you see, my own sacred springtime. She ruined it forever."

"Child, child, you're forgetting again, the tree fell only on you. But she'll come back to visit us again, don't worry. Or I'll go visit her, if you don't feel up to it."

"And what will you tell her?"

◆

The truth. I told her the truth. That I thought she was a very interesting character. It was a good argument because she, I could tell right away, is also convinced that she's a very interesting character. She likes to be the protagonist; there's no doubt about that. I noticed she was very curious to find out how I would describe her. In her own way, she told me everything, in an animated voice and with a foreign accent; in short, with the cadences and expressions of her adopted country; no one listening to her would say she's an Argentine. She knows how to manipulate certain facts, but she's clever: she doesn't play the martyr. Quite the opposite. I brought her a newspaper article that mentions the Shark; the reporter, perhaps intending to add another scurrilous nuance to the description of a torturer, or with the intention of doing her justice, wrote that the Shark had seduced a prisoner. When she read it, she became furious: "Nobody ever seduced me," she said proudly. "I was always the seducer." It must be true. She tried to seduce me, too. And I admit she sometimes succeeded. She's very strong. I was going to say "passionate," but it's just an imitation of passion; she's cold and calculating at heart. A dangerous woman. I suppose she'll enjoy that description. She also said, "I know several women who slept with the members of the Task Force, but I," pointing to her chest, "I loved the Shark." She uses the word love quite a bit. She loved the Shark, she loved the father of her child, she loved the gorgeous guerrilla leader with whom she deceived the father of her child: by the way, she told me a long story where mad love combines with military operations in which her own life is endangered and where people are killed, and where the father of her child, setting his military scruples aside, holds a gun to his temple and threatens to kill himself, but all this is another story. She loved that revolutionary leader, she loved the teenage boyfriend who wanted to go to Officer Training School, she loved – loves – her current husband, a tall man with noble, Indian good looks, who every so often served us coffee and looked after the baby. The baby wasn't born of her own womb; she's adopted, although after listening to her speak for three straight days, I'm prepared to swear that, if she didn't give birth on the threshold of her fiftieth birthday, it's because she didn't resolutely decide to do so. She proudly showed me pictures of her wedding. Naturally she got married in church, and naturally she wore white; her smile was as wide and as happy as in the photos of her graduation trip to Mendoza and in the photo she gave me, where you see her looking radiant beside Queen Genevieve at the Luxemburgo. Life is inexhaustible, she said to me, without a trace of irony. She's quite interested in the political situation in her adopted country, "the country of my younger daughter and my husband," she said. "Although he's not interested in politics," she added, slightly scornfully. "All he cares about is us." Right now, she explained, she's working on a high-level political project. She told me about that project with the same fervour she used, I imagine, at Communist Party meetings or at university assemblies or at guerrilla indoctrination sessions. With the same effusiveness she used to harangue her innocent classmates at the Normal School and to

177

expound her proposals to the Admiral. I left when the baby started crying. It's true, I said to myself, life is inexhaustible. It wasn't a happy thought. It was, let's say, a thought without a sign. And the bad thing is that we were made for a world with signs; the traitorous pirate buried up to his neck, waiting for the tide to come in, the purest among us at the helm of a revolution of human dimensions. It's not such an easy thing. And yet, there she was still, a few yards from Café Mecca, the Little Match Girl, dragging her snot-nosed little brother by the hand and looking at me with a certain contempt.

As I walked very quickly away from that house, it occurred to me that an unwitting spectator, watching the window across the way from the roof of the Mecca, might have thought that the olive-skinned, somewhat voluptuous woman, who at that moment was intently feeding her baby, was born to drink life down to the bottom of the glass. It doesn't really matter, I said to myself. That isn't always a virtue.

ABOUT THE AUTHOR

Liliana Heker was born in 1943 in Buenos Aires, Argentina. She is the author of two novels and many books of short stories and essays, in addition to being a founder of two important Argentine literary magazines. Her collected short stories were published in Spanish in 2004 and translated into Hebrew; her stories have been included in anthologies in many countries and languages. Her collection, *The Stolen Party and Other Stories*, is available in English.

The End of the Story was not only a literary success, but a cultural event that provoked controversy and avid discussion of how best to remember the years of the Argentine dictatorship.

ABOUT THE TRANSLATOR

Andrea G. Labinger has translated novels by numerous Latin American writers, including Luisa Valenzuela, Sabina Berman, Alicia Steimberg and Ana María Shua. She holds a Ph.D. in Latin American Literature from Harvard University and is Professor Emerita of Spanish at the University of La Verne, California.